Julia Summerland • Love in Times of Coronavirus II

To Katarina and Maurice

This second book of Julia Summerland's novel is highly addictive. The highs and lows she goes through with all the potential Mr. Rights make for an incredible reading experience. And now I'm feeling torn, because I want her to find "the one", but on the other hand I don't want her to ever stop writing about her funny stories.

(Katarina)

Julia Summerland

LOVE IN TIMES OF CORONAVIRUS II

My crazy dating in the shadow of the pandemic

With the exception of public figures, all the characters depicted in this book are creatures of Julia's imagination and any resemblance to any real person is coincidental. However, the events around the Covid-19 pandemic in 2020 and 2021 were very real and are described as they happened.

Bibliographic Information of the German National Library
The German National Library has registered this publication
in the German National Bibliography;
detailed bibliographic information can be found online at http://dnb.d-nb.de.
© Edition AVRA: A trademark of Frieling & Huffmann GmbH & Co. KG
Phone: 0 30 / 766 999-0
www.frieling.de
Cover illustration: Emilia Agovic
Image source: pixabay
1st Edition 2021
ISBN (print) 978-3-8280-3637-6
ISBN (e-book) 978-3-8280-3638-3
All rights reserved Printed in Germany

CONTENTS

THINGS ARE STILL HECTIC 8

AUTUMN APPROACHES 28

A NEW NORMAL? 36

TIME FOR A TALK 51

MEETING YOUR LOVE 62

HOMEWRECKER, DESTROYER OF WORLDS 91

FRIENDS SAVE THE DAY 109

LOVE IN TIMES OF... 121

Preface by Bernard

What do they know? Men are funny animals.

Summerland has done it again! In her new novel, Summerland questions human nature, and specifically the nature of the 'worse half' of humanity, men. Like little kids they are good at playing with their toys, from their phones to their new electric Hummer cars, from the mountain bikes to their forty foot yachts. But what do they know about what is happening in their immediate families, circle of friends, around them and just under their nose?

This story describes the complex relationship between husband and wife and a father and his children, from the point of view of the man's lover. Not just any lover, but a lover in Corona times, when physical contact is limited and even seeing each other is sanctioned by the state which 'closes and opens' people's life. Moreover, the story takes place in Luxembourg, a small place where everybody knows everybody else and any secretive escapade becomes public knowledge within days.

Who knew, what and when? Reading Summerland's new book will create as many questions as it provides answers. Why are men so oblivious to their most intimate relationships? Are they born like that? Good at hunting but bad in nursing? Multiplying their genetic code to ensure the continuity of their own genotype? Does it have to do with the fact that they are raised by mothers who make sure their sons would be totally dependent on them for growing up? Or does it have to do with the way society expects men to behave differently than women, be macho, tough and never cry, depend on the other gender to support their basic needs, and only be responsible to get enough dough on the family table?

It is an intriguing story, full of laughter and amusement, just the right reading stuff for a long pandemic season.

Bernard M.

THINGS ARE STILL HECTIC

"Life does not always write the best stories. However, it writes the most honest ones."

(Katarina)

***

A long time ago – in March 2020 to be exact – when people did not need to wear masks and could do all kinds of things without social distancing, I found myself at a crossroad in my life.

After a treasured relationship had been ended by my long-term partner I was feeling a little aimless and drifting when the first coronavirus lockdown began and this galvanised me. There was only one thing to do: find the man of my dreams in spite of what was happening and what might happen.

I decided that the best way to achieve this goal would be to sign up to an online dating platform called Meetyourlove. The men I met there and the stories I heard inspired me to write a book about my experiences.

That first book– 'Love in Times of Coronavirus' – concluded on 14 July 2020 – after just five hectic months when the world seemed to have turned upside down.

I continue the story from then.

Carl, Alan, Jordan

On 6 August 2020, my first book – 'Love in Times of Coronavirus' – went to print.

It was a hot and dry summer day. Temperatures had been well above thirty degrees for weeks without rain, which is exceptional for Luxembourg. Very unusually, from the first lockdown in March 2020, the sun had come out and had stayed all spring and all summer long.

At this point, there were mainly three men in my life, all three asking me out on that same day. However, none of these three men seemed to be suitable partner material. Earlier in the year, I had joined the online dating platform meetyourlove.org with the purpose of meeting a suitable partner.

So far, my efforts had not been successful, upended by the coronavirus pandemic right at the beginning of my first encounters, with social distancing measures, lockdown, the air becoming so clean and colours really beautiful; not to mention closures of restaurants, bars, shops, borders, and curfews and having to stay close to home, all to reduce infection, loss of work, and airplanes on the ground. Writing down the meetings with the different men helped me overcome my sorrow but the right man remained elusive and that's why I continued writing about my experiences.

These three men were, in August 2020: Carl (married), Alan (my ex), and Jordan (too old for me).

That day, the first to call me was Carl.

"Do you want to go for a bike ride this afternoon with me, before my race with the group? Tonight we are meeting with the group in Contern. We could meet in Hesperange park and from there we could cycle together to Contern. The road is partially closed to cars over the summer, which makes it a nice ride."

"Very good idea," I replied, "Let's do it!"

The second was Alan.

"Do you want to go for a bike ride today, after work?" Alan asked me.

"Six or half past would be perfect."

"Maybe a bit earlier, five thirty?"

"Sorry, busy then."

"Shall we meet in Hesperange park and do the bike path together?

"Perfect!"

The third was Jordan.

"Julia," he asked, "do you want to come for dinner tonight at my place, melon with ham, what time could you come?"

"Eight would be good for me, right after my Distance Fitness!" (I had created Distance Fitness on 19 March 2020 as a response to the full lockdown. It offered people socially-distanced fitness classes from their balconies or in the courtyard of my apartment building.)

That same hot, summer evening, after having met with all three men, I sat on my balcony and reflected on my life, my attempts to find the right partner, my failure to do so, coronavirus, my writing, my teaching, climate change, online dating, and, most importantly, the possibility of going on holiday in coronavirus times.

Coronavirus restrictions were eased and many travel restrictions were lifted, with the result that people travelled and got infected and there were rising numbers of infections.
With partial closures, there were quarantines.
Luxembourg was on the list of dangerous countries to travel to and people coming from Luxembourg had to quarantine for 14 days when travelling to Germany.

August: time for a getaway

Shortly after awakening, I, spontaneously but decisively, packed my things and went on a week's holiday to the Holland region and Amsterdam. I had been to North Holland before with Alan. We used to travel there several times a year. Still, since he had left me I hadn't returned to the place I loved so much. Now, this morning, I suddenly felt ready to face it and the memories.

Everything was as nice as always in Holland. There was however one exception: the weather was extremely hot. It is rare to see the region so hot with the fields dried out, with sunburnt grass.

I wrote to Alan on WhatsApp, "I am in Holland." He answered, "Don't write or call, please, I am with, you know." He was with his new girlfriend, the one he had left me for. He was so afraid of the new girl's jealousy.

On arrival, the big change was the 'normality' of the place. Coronavirus? What coronavirus? Here in North Holland, it was not very visible, besides face masks on public transport. Nobody wore them on their bikes. This was a welcome change.

There was one thing I had wished to do for years and had never dared: the Texel skydive, a tandem jump from 13,000 feet. I went to the Texel airport by ferryboat and bike. I stood there, watching the others jump. I took videos and photos but didn't jump. I returned to my hotel, frustrated.

Carl wrote: "Did you do it?"

"No, sorry, maybe another time."

I felt so bad about this that the next day I registered for a jump. There was not a single cloud in the sky.

That day, I did the Skydive at Texel.

It was fantastic!

Absolutely amazing.

The view from 13,000 feet was breath-taking, so was the free fall. My instructor, a young blond woman as well, opened the parachute and we glided softly to earth. The views over the island were absolutely astounding, everything seemed so calm from up there. No more problems. They had all vanished at the moment I jumped out of the plane, with the wind's noise in my ears and my arms spread out. The instructor showed me what to do, how to behave, what to do next and how to steer the parachute. The landing, ah, the landing was smooth and soft on the grass. Coronavirus rules still applied though, everybody had to jump with their face masks on.

Carl was curious, "How was it?" he asked. He rarely telephoned, normally he preferred to write, but now he wanted to hear the story with his own ears. "It was absolutely amazing…" I breathed. Finally, I had got some admiration, I noticed, some actual admiration from Carl.

Carl wanted to know, "How high is 13,000 feet? Your feet or my feet? This would make a difference!"

"I think it is something around 4,000 metres."

"When did you open the parachute? At what height?"

"Honestly, I don't know."

Jordan wrote: "Now this is my Julia, just how I love her! When shall we jump together? You are the best and will always be the best for me! I am ready to jump together with you! But how high is 13,000 feet?"

The dating game

I cycled the bike path from Bergen to Den Helder, via Schoorl and Callantsog, through the dunes and taking the lovely rolling path. Then it was back from Den Helder to Bergen-aan-Zee, with a stop in Callantsog to eat kibbeling and kippers at the fish restaurant. Arriving in Bergen-aan-Zee through the dunes with the smell of the pine forest was unforgettable. Then after that, there was the joy of swimming in the North Sea. At first, the water seemed bitingly cold, but then, once in the water, I noticed how warm the water itself was in that heat. It was fun to enjoy the waves and to laugh and shout like everybody else. Then it was time for sunbathing on the fine white sand. But how unusually crowded it was, it had never been so crowded there before. Well, the fine weather must have made everybody come to this beach. Indeed, the beach was packed with families, kids and parents playing happily in the sand, building sandcastles, and collecting shells or simply strolling along the beach.

Tomorrow it would be back to Luxembourg, unfortunately the week's holiday was already coming to an end.

In the evening, in my hotel room, I suddenly felt horribly lonesome. There are such moments. Despite having been brave and courageous all of these days, all of a sudden, I felt alone – and took to Meetyourlove. Why not?

Carl, Alan and Jordan wouldn't know.

I found this man: smiling, good looking, sporty. I gave him my phone number. He wrote a WhatsApp message: "Hallo, I am the man from Meetyourlove. Thank you for your number."

"What's your real name?"

"My name is Pat, I am from Munich originally, and have been working in Luxembourg for 20 years."

"Very nice to hear from you, you speak German then?"

"Yes."

And this was the end of the conversation for this evening. "Strange," I thought.

The next day, Sunday 16 August, it was twenty-seven degrees in Amsterdam at seven in the morning. The streets were empty, most people would have gone to bed just a few hours ago after enjoying their Saturday night out. I packed and left for Luxembourg. The drive back home was uneventful besides one funny curiosity. It rained exactly, really exactly, at the border sign showing 'Luxembourg'. A thunderstorm burst right there, unbelievable. All through the Netherlands and Belgium the weather had been perfect.

Carl messaged me: "Good morning Julia. Kisses."

"If you want to kiss me in person this afternoon..."

Carl: ":)"

And that was the end of the conversation with Carl for the day. "Strange," I thought again.

Jordan also messaged me: "Good morning dear Julia, I hope you enjoy your performance in the air for a long time, yes forever! Yesterday was a holiday in Luxembourg. I did a bike tour from Ettelbruck passing by Echternach to Wasserbillig, about 50km. The train was packed with people and bikes....Kisses. Jordan."

I messaged back: "Hello Jordan. I am back home."

Jordan got on the phone and called me. We talked a while about the day, just a nice normal phone conversation.

Later I took my bike for a short ride on the bike path to Hesperange and back.

Jordan wrote: "I have too many mirabelle plums, may I come to bring you some this evening? Kisses. Jordan."

"Yes please, after half past seven, I am teaching an online class before then."

"Ok, I'll be at your place at eight-thirty."

Next, there was a message from Pat: "Good day!"

"Thank you, you too," I sent back.

Pat: "Nice to hear from you."

"What are you up to?"

"Just at home, relaxing. And you?"

"I'm cycling."

"You are very sporty!"

"Not you?" I asked.

He concluded with: "Enjoy!"

And that was it. He was short in his messages. Not really talkative, was he?

Back from the bike ride, I again took to Meetyourlove.

There was a man, Markus, who had contacted me the day before, but I hadn't replied straight away. So I looked at his details and photos. I liked what I saw. Not too old, close to my age, sporty and divorced. Ah, divorced, hopefully it's true. Kids, yes. "Ok," I thought. I liked him back, he replied, instantly, with his email address. "He must be decisive to answer so fast." I emailed him with my phone number, so that he could contact me via WhatsApp.

Markus: "It is my pleasure to write to you. If it's okay, I'll call you after dinner."

"Enjoy your dinner! Yes, please call me after dinner!"

Markus: "I'll call you at eight-thirty."

No! This was the exact same time that Jordan had said he would arrive with the mirabelles.

Indeed, Jordan rang the doorbell exactly on time, the same time that Markus called. I opened the door for Jordan, with the phone in my hand, replying to Markus: "Hello Markus, how are you? Nice talking to you, may I call you back in a moment. I'm just having a friend visiting?"

"Yes, no problem, please call me back later."

Jordan brought his mirabelles and some pastries for next morning's breakfast. We talked a while and after he had left, I called Markus back.

"Hello Markus, how are you? Nice talking to you!"

"So, Julia, you are sports instructor?"

"Well, coronavirus has changed my agenda, let's say, I was sports instructor before. Now I am teaching more languages and university than sports."

"Ah, yes, coronavirus has changed a lot our lives…"

And so the conversation went on. Just a normal phone call, until we said good night and Markus added, "I'll send you a picture with me in my sports team, you can guess who I am in the picture and tell me tomorrow morning!"

I went to sleep.

Next morning, I checked my messages and yes Markus had sent the group picture. I guessed who he was, first row on the right. He also sent a photo of a rose from his garden, a red rose, for me.

I thought, "Very nice, very kind," and wrote: "Thank you for the nice rose!"

The two of us continued chatting all morning and arranged to phone in the evening.

In the morning, Alan sent a message.

Alan: "Hope you are well?"

I sent him a long text: "Fine thanks. I'm now back in Luxembourg. I did a skydive in Texel, you remember, the parachute jump you never dared to do. This time, I jumped and not only did I survive it, it was amazing! I also went swimming in the North Sea, which we never did as the water always was too cold. Emotionally, it was important to me to do this trip. Since you left me, I couldn't visit that part of Holland. We always went there together. It was you who introduced me to this our heaven on earth. Now I felt strong enough to return, alone, and enjoy it as much as I had enjoyed it for all these years together with you. I went to Amsterdam and to Haarlem, just like we used to do. Thank you for having shown me this. By the way, yesterday, on Meetyourlove, I met a serious, sporty man. Will tell you more later. Julia."

Alan: "Be careful on Meetyourlove, don't trust anybody. In Holland these were extraordinary unforgettable moments together, to be honest, me too I cry when I think about those special moments, but as said, life cannot only be this! Do you understand? I'll never have those weeks in Holland back."

Carl also contacted me.

Carl: "Good morning Julia, did you sleep well? How are you? Kisses."

"You didn't have time to answer my message yesterday?"

Carl: "Sorry."

"You could have at least answered, saying you have no time, or how are you, do you need anything? Did you have a nice trip? But nothing from your side. I am not an ice lady, you know."

Friends and books

Tuesday night was Distance Fitness, the class that I taught outside in my courtyard for the women of the neighbourhood, and since Jasmine and Jordan always attended, I was nervous and curious to see Jordan's reaction to my new book.

But I needn't have worried because Jordan said, "You did well, very well. You wrote this book wonderfully! Hahahaha, when I realised you had written it, I had such a huge laugh in my kitchen, just outstanding. You succeed in surprising me every time!"

"When did you realise that the book was about us, about you, about Luxembourg?" I asked.

"Well, I started reading in the middle, with the bike ride to Trier, and then the other one to Munsbach castle with the flowers in the garden, I thought, this is too much coincidence, this is about us! Hahahaha, you did this so well. And the part when I grab the cigarette butts to throw them in the bin, and when I ask you to marry me and be part of my family. This is a serious offer and it still stands and is still valid, and will always be valid, this is serious! Hahahaha, how you describe this, really funny! Now I have to read the entire book from the beginning!"

On Friday, Carl and I met to go cycling in Terre Rouge – Red Rock – as usual just after lunch. The Schifflange cemetery was our meeting point. The ride through the forest was quiet and we took in the many sights. The soil was, as advertised, red, the trees green and the sky blue with just the right amount of clouds. As usual, we ended our ride at the 'Venus plateau', the place with the view over Belval University. As we both cherished this place, I chose it as the right place to give Carl my new book.

He looked at the title and said, "Oh, Love in Times of Coronavirus. You find this book interesting because of the nice things we did together during that time."

"Yes. But you'll just put it away with the other book I gave you weeks ago without reading it! Don't put it away unread!"

On the same Friday evening, my mother called via Skype, holding the book in her hands with a big smile in her face.

"Look, your book has arrived! It really looks good! Thank you so much! I started reading, but in English, this will take me a little longer!"

I told my mother about Jordan's reaction to the book.

"Now I am curious to see Carl's reaction, if there is any. He probably won't read it at all but put it away somewhere."

"We will see, this is funny!" my mother said, laughing.

"Yes, this is really funny, especially because you had advised me NOT to show them the book at all. Now it's done, it's good that I gave them the book and I was honest."

Jordan

"Good night, my darling. Are you already asleep? I would have liked to talk a bit with you. Reading your book, I reached Louis' story. The last sentences by Alan must have hurt you deeply, oh, there are very sad moments in life, sometimes I ask myself: how long can one stand such sadness? I admire your strength to overcome these sad moments. I saw there were flowers on the bridge, the Pont Adolphe, I suppose another suicide, this makes me so sad. Since I read your book, I understand how little sense life makes without love. We are not made for being alone. I understand you perfectly and love you even more, the more I read your story the more I love you. Good night, your Jordan."

Carl

Carl and I went mountain biking in the Red Rock area.

After the dry summer, the trees were losing their leaves early this year. The ground was covered with dry leaves. It was twenty-two degrees – warm but much, much less than last week. We felt the autumn approaching. It seemed so early.

I asked, "Carl, did you read the book I gave you?"

"No, not yet."

"Where do you have it? On the dining table?"

"No, with a title like that, 'Love in Times of Coronavirus', I prefer keeping it wrapped in its paper in my backpack."

"You'd better bring it back to me tomorrow, I forgot something."

"Okay."

The following day he arrived with the book and said, "I brought back your book. But I still don't know why."

"Just like that."

"But why? I'll not show it to my wife or children."

With a big smile on his face he continued, "I'll not leave it on the living room table either. So, why should I have brought it back?"

"No particular reason, just wanted to say, you could read it while on holiday next week."

"Don't worry, I'll not show it anybody at home. It's safe with me."

With a big smile, Carl continued cycling.

I also had a big smile, especially because I knew Carl hadn't read the book yet, nor had he even skimmed it. Otherwise, he would not have spoken that way. This was funny.

Later, after our bike ride, I asked again, "Do you still have my book in your backpack?"

"Yes, I do, it didn't fly away, don't worry, I'll keep it safe from my family."

"Good," I replied, "you could read it while on holiday next week."

I thought, he is not going to look at it at all; just like the other book I had given him.

So funny.

Jasmine

The same evening, there was Distance Fitness with Jordan and Jasmine and Toby and Peter and Carmen. It was the moment for me to give Jasmine my book. Together with Jordan we took pictures of the very moment. Jasmine was so intuitive, she looked at the book and asked, "You wrote this book, didn't you?"

It had taken her not even one second to size up the situation. She understood it all.

I hesitated and said, "Oh, no, I just thought you would like to have it. Let me write you a dedication... Okay, yes, yes, you with your female intuition, you noticed it from the beginning that I'm the author."

"I am so excited," said Jasmine, "I'll read and finish it by Friday, I'm so curious!"

AUTUMN APPROACHES

It was still warm but autumn was coming. Carl and I went for a bike ride and also to eat fresh plums and ripe apples from the trees. We stopped at one street where twenty years ago a fruit tree was planted for each new birth in the village. We picked the fruit and ate them fresh from the trees. Other people were doing the same. At the end of the bike ride, we went to our favourite spot to sit and watch the sun go down over Belval, with a lovely sunset glow around us.

I thought, "Autumn is coming. The corn fields are harvested, the plums are ripe, and soon the grapes will be ripe in the Moselle valley. The days are getting definitely shorter and it's getting cooler."

Carl hadn't looked at the book yet at all. How could I make him read the book without being too pushy? I would try to tell him again to read it next week during his holiday.

The same day, Jordan wrote a message: "Hi dear Julia, maybe we could have a bike ride today or tomorrow afternoon. Kisses, my Julia, Jordan in love."

Markus, who I had met on Meetyourlove.org, continued to send messages with flowers. I thought, "He lives too far away. This makes no sense. He never sends pictures of himself. When video calling, he only has the audio on, never the video. There must be something wrong with his looks, why else would he hide so much? And these flowers, every day flowers, well, I love flowers, but this seems a bit exaggerated."

Thursday, 27 August 2020

For a Zoom webinar about time management for university, I had over two hundred attendees in Pakistan. The first webinar about this had been held in July with participants mainly from Egypt. The next would be in September in Kenya.

I had many more ideas for webinars.

Friday, 28 August 2020

Jordan

"Good Morning dear Julia, if one day you should get ill or if you feel unwell, I am always there for you! Just call me! Being alone in a difficult situation is horrible and awful. Take care. I love you. Jordan."

Carl

Carl came to see me, bringing cakes to go with the tea.

"You can take the book with you on holiday," I suggested.

"You know, last time on holidays I took a book with me and you know how much I read of it? Not one single page. Why? Every morning we were on our bikes by nine then we rode all day. When we got back, we were tired, we ate and went to sleep. There is no time for reading books."

"Okay, I see."

Carl turned the Australian rainmaker that I had brought back from one of my trips.

In the evening there was Distance Fitness with Jasmine, Jordan and all the others.

It started raining heavily, a real storm.

I later wrote to Carl: "You know, the rainmaker works! You turned it and it rained, the first time in weeks that it has rained!"

Saturday, 29 August 2020

I received this message from Jordan: "Good morning Julia, how nice that you write to me to wish me a nice day early in the morning. In fact I had no rain during my ride back but drops began to hit me on the last bit, I accelerated and arrived dry. Then it bucketed down. After a busy day I fell into bed at 23:45 and could not help but read your book. I was awake again and read until 00:45. I enjoyed your lovely description of all that unique 3000 km biking experience with Carl. I felt happy when reading how you enjoyed the strawberry waffle, the best in your life so far. Glad that you took advantage of those unique conditions, now I am even more motivated for buying a racing bike. Enjoy your day, my darling, kisses your Jordan."

I wrote to Carl: "Wishing you a great trip. The weather will be nice, warm, no snow, did you take the book with you?"

There were many more new cases of coronavirus in France, with over 7000 new infections in one day. In Germany, there were 1500 new cases per day. Would there soon be a vaccine? The Tour de France started in Nizza in the midst of increasing coronavirus infections in France. There were limits on the number of spectators and mask wearing was mandatory.

Sunday, 30 August 2020

Jordan, Peter, Jasmine and I went biking on this last August weekend. During this coronavirus summer several roads were closed to cars every weekend. On Saturday, the day before, I had tried out one of the routes, the one that goes from Mamer to Mersch through the forest. I wanted to be sure that when riding it with my friends, it would be enjoyable for everybody, not too difficult, not too easy either, just the right distance. It was about forty kilometres long and mainly on the bike path through the forest and over the fields. Luckily the weather was still fine and warm, with rain forecast for the evening.

Indeed, everybody enjoyed this Sunday on the bikes, with a fine picnic at the end in Parc Laval in the sun.

"Do you want some milk?" Jordan asked Peter.

"With pleasure!" Peter replied.

"Do you also want a Kamell?"

"A what?"

"Kamell, that's the Luxembourgish word for a sweet. You will get it only if you pronounce it correctly in your best Luxembourgish."

"Kamell, Kamell, Kamell," Peter repeated several times.

On the way back, Jordan asked, "Shall we take the elevator?"

"Yes," replied Jasmine, "That's faster and easier. From there we can ride through the park."

While cycling through the park, Jasmine asked, "How about we go on the Ferris wheel at the fair? I would very much enjoy taking it and it would be a nice end to our Sunday."

"Yes, please, we only live once!" said Peter.

And off we went to ride on the big wheel, with its great views over Luxembourg city in the setting sun.

Monday, 31 August 2020

Alan

"I had a long talk with my son. He thinks I should not hide my friendship with you to my new girlfriend. He says either I stop my friendship with you or I have to tell her about it. It is not right to continue seeing you and dating her."

I replied, "What I wish is friendship with you. Nothing more, nothing less."

"He thinks I should not see you anymore. I think he's right. It is not right to have a friendship with you."

"Well, I need to see you to give you something. Let's meet today, after work?"

I had planned to give Alan my book and see his reaction to it.

Later, while I was on the way on my bike, Alan messaged me to say that he was not coming because of the weather and because he was having dinner with his children.

He suggested giving up our friendship to save his current relationship. I thought that was outrageous. I would never give up any friendship because somebody else asked me to do so. I stand up for my friendships. But not everybody does, I would learn.

Carl, on holiday, sent quite a few messages with photos and videos.

Jordan came to see me in the evening to check if I was okay. He was worried as I hadn't given any sign of life.

A NEW NORMAL?

Tuesday, 1 September 2020

Alan told me that his relationship with his children was difficult because of his rapport with different women.

Jordan sent emails with flowers.

Carl sent photos of himself and his bike, his friends and beautiful landscapes.

This year, there was no Schueberfouer, the annual fair in Luxembourg, because of the coronavirus pandemic. However there were some stands spread all over town, more or less well-visited.

In the Tour de France Julian Alaphilippe won the yellow jersey with many tears shed. Julian Alaphilippe's father has passed away in June.

Luxembourg coronavirus numbers:
124 deaths in Luxembourg
6673 infections
Reproduction number: 1.03
New infections per day: 7.67 people per 100,000 people.

Thursday, 3 September 2020

The new program for Sports pour Tous arrived. I needed to decide which ones to teach but at that point in my life I wanted more free time to be creative. It didn't seem an easy choice.

Summer was definitely over, along with my time on the bike with Carl.

Since the lockdown began on 13 March, I had cycled 5000 kilometres in Luxembourg, nearly every afternoon on my bike. Now this extraordinary time was over. Definitely over. It was just a dream.

Sadness took hold of me. Real sadness, this had been a period with so much free time.

Now, if I wanted to have some free time, I needed to give up some income.

I called Alan.

He said, "From tomorrow on, I'll be with my girlfriend for one week. Don't call me, don't write to me on WhatsApp, write to me on Viber." He added, "This is very good, you are lucky: you have the choice to choose your classes. You have so much work. Imagine, how lucky you are. Take them all, take all your classes back."

Jordan wrote, "Good night my darling. Love you."

"Unquestionably, 'Coronavirus times' are over. It's back to normality," I thought.

My Distance Fitness would stop in a week. The normal sports classes put on by the town councils were due to restart, so there was no need for Distance Fitness any longer.

The Pilates class in Roeser was cancelled because of increasing coronavirus cases.

The Frankfurter Book Fair was cancelled for the same reason.

In California, there were huge forest fires, with the air turning orange at night, the smoke being so dense that the Golden Gate Bridge was no longer to be seen. Climate change was to be seen everywhere. There was low rainfall everywhere it seemed.
Many countries may not be liveable in the future.
Climate migrants may be a reality
Would the future be one of water scarcity, migration and food shortage?

Thursday, 10 September 2020

Alan

I was attending an online conference when Alan called. He was in town, not too far away, and said he would come to pick up his present. He parked in front of my apartment.

I gave him my book.

"Why did you put on such red lipstick?"

"It's because of the online conference. If I put on my usual lipstick, it is not visible online. They told me to put on a darker one that can be seen better."

He unwrapped the book and started reading. "Oh, Luxembourg? This is set in Luxembourg? I'll read it tonight. First, I'll go cycling and then I'll read it."

"You could start reading directly and then you will not go to cycling anymore."

"No, I'll read it after."

"You could read it in one hour."

"In Italian, yes, but it is in English, I need a bit more time."

"Enjoy the reading, bye, I have to go to my conference now."

That evening he wrote: "Who is Julia Summerland?!!!!"

One minute later he added: "You are Julia and I am Alan!"

It had taken him three hours to start reading the book. He wrote: "You put me into a state of feeling that I cannot explain. Please call me asap. I don't feel well, I cannot sleep."

Carl

In the meantime, Carl had not even opened the book after three weeks. I had given Carl the book on Friday 21 July. He hadn't opened it at all so far, despite many heavy hints. He ignored all of these attempts to make him even notice it.

"Interesting behaviour," I thought, astonishingly interesting.

"Why doesn't he look at the two books I've given him?"

Is he not curious at all to read what is written in the books?

Is he afraid of the content?

Does he think he knows what it's about?

Why doesn't he read the books?

Really, why doesn't he read them? Does he want the situation to remain how it is, unchanged? Does he not want to see what is written? Is he simply procrastinating? I really had no idea.

Jordan

I wrote to Jordan: "How are you?"

Jordan: "I have the impression you want more distance from me I feel lonely and think at a lot of what I read in your book. I think I need to join Meetyourlove as well. Both of our lives seem to have reached a decisive moment. The worst for me is not knowing what really is in our friendship. We don't have enough time to exchange what really goes on in our heads, that is the source of doubt and despair on my side. In addition, along comes Covid-19 where not a single real kiss is allowed. And the virtual ones seem to fade away...Anyway, I'll always love you! You had a great impact on my life, I got more spontaneous and began biking again. Thankfulness is a great value to me. Therefore my love to you is real and steady, sustainable in a more modern speech. You can always rely on it. Whatever decision you have taken or will take. Maybe this is all imagination, I simply do not know. Please Julia, let me know. Good night, kisses, Jordan."

Friday, 11 September 2020

Six months ago, a lockdown was declared in Luxembourg.

The fires in California and Oregon have destroyed so much forest. Climate change and global heating was the reason. It hadn't rained for years there. In Luxembourg, it didn't rain for months. The weather was still sunny and warm, which was unusual for mid-September.

Alan

Alan said, "Julia, you should no longer be on these online dating sites. You should unregister yourself. You are with Carl now. In every relationship, there are things that are not a hundred percent perfect. However, you should not be looking for another man."

Other friends of mine had told me the same, saying that the sites were not good for me.

Alan added, "You know, we had the best time of our lives, I'll never again have such moments like with you. We travelled the world, and if somebody asks me with whom I would like to travel to the Netherlands, I would answer with Julia, or to Kenya, with Julia, to Australia, with Julia. However in day-to-day life, we would not have got along. You have this need for freedom and independence, you don't have the need for being together with me all the time. Therefore it is impossible for us to continue.

Also, you always go to bed so early. Even on Christmas Eve you go to bed at ten. People joke about you because you always go to sleep so early and you never deviate from this. Also, I was so jealous about your past. It was unbearable, intolerable, this jealousy made me suffer so much, I couldn't stand it any longer. Now, I don't have this feeling anymore, so I feel better."

Jordan

I sent Jordan a message: "Today there is more free time, so I have time to talk. Two-thirty at your place?"

Jordan: "Okay, I have had better days, but I am happy to talk. Let's go to the park and sit in the sun."

Once seated on a bench in the park he said, "Please, Julia, I love you so much. It is so difficult for me to like and then to love somebody, it takes a lot of time for me to open up, to like somebody, to make a person come into my heart, but once there, this person is there for ever. I love you so much."

"You know that I love another man. I suggest we stay very good friends, if this is okay for everybody. It would be the best solution for all of us."

"My fear was that you would say we should not see each other anymore."

"Why would I say such a thing? We are such good friends and it is important to have good friends."

Carl

Early in the morning, Carl went for a long mountain bike ride with a friend.

Normally, he writes or sends pictures, but not today, so I messaged him in the afternoon.

"Everything fine with you?"

Carl wrote back: "I hurt my right hand in a fall."

He continued with a video call. He was standing next to a lake close to his home in the forest. The water in the lake was very low because of the lack of rain.

"Look, this is my hand, my thumb is getting blue, it hurts, and also a scratch here on my leg, luckily I was wearing my knee pads and long sleeves, so nothing else happened."

"If your hand is okay, do you think we still can go mountain biking tomorrow afternoon? Let's pick some plums, and see if the nuts are ripe, go explore the Red Rock area, the butterfly trail and the nice green forests, and the views over the valley and the trails. This would be my plan."

We continued talking, then Carl left for home and I went to my Pilates Skype class and the very last lesson of Distance Fitness.

The last Distance Fitness?

After six months of Distance Fitness, this was the final edition. In-person lessons would begin again soon, life was back to normal, or nearly normal.

Jasmine, Catherine, Jordan, Peter and I were there and Jasmine had a present for me. Jasmine and Jordan stayed long after to talk. Distance Fitness had been there for us for six months. It had been a special type of sports during a special time.

However, with rising coronavirus cases in France and also in Luxembourg, all of this was unstable and unsure. The future was uncertain.

Carl

"How are you?"

Carl: "I prefer to stay at home."

Sunday, 13 September 2020

Marlon

Despite Alan's recommendation not to go on Meetyourlove anymore, from time to time I looked at the site to check what was going on, who had viewed my profile, who did what, who wrote, who was in the 'Shuffle', and maybe get a phone call.

This is how I rediscovered Marlon, a former colleague of mine.

"It is because of you that I enrolled on Meetyourlove. I wanted to know what happened to you, how you are and what you are up to."

He certainly had had an interesting time on the site and told me a few stories.

"I once found a woman on the website," he began, "it was a stormy day, and so I suggested we could go for a walk instead of going for a drink. She came to my apartment and parked in the street. They always say one should not meet in the apartment for the first time, so I went down to the street to her car. She stepped out of the car and had so high heels on and a long skirt. 'Where will she be going to walk to with this outfit?' So we walked a bit and came to a small bridge, and she said 'I cannot walk over this bridge!' 'Yes, I thought, you cannot walk over this bridge.' So we came back to her car and she drove away. Ah, yes, she also wanted to go on holiday with me. I said, 'With pleasure, if you pay for it.'"

On Meetyourlove there are so many women who are only looking for money, nothing else. They want me to take them out for dinner, or for a holiday, and I should pay.

On another site, I noticed, they have these people that pretend to be a woman, but they are a gang. The story is always the same. They write, and when you start getting interested, they say they want to come to see you by plane, and then the mother falls ill and they ask for money to be sent. I always let the conversation go until this stage and then I tell them to go to hell. I'm on different platforms at the same time and am in contact with over 20 women."

We got to talking about Carl and he said, "You really seem to like your Carl. How can we make him leave his wife? He cannot stay married all the time, that's not a good situation."

"I have an idea. Next time I am with him, you call her at home, on her landline. That should be simple," I suggested, "She could be your woman. You are looking for a new woman, here is one for you! She would be free, as he is with me. What do you think?"

"Hahahaha, that's the best idea ever. Even for Meetyourlove this would be a novelty."

Ulrich

Ulrich had contacted me on Meetyourlove. He was divorced, had two children and had been on the site for only a few weeks. Because of coronavirus, he preferred to play it safe and not to meet too many women in person. In fact, he had only met one woman before me. Three days later, Ulrich wrote to me asking to stop the conversation and to delete all his contact details.

Fabien

Previously, he had been very sporty, but then injured himself in 2016 and didn't exercise anymore. No more bike rides, no jogging, nothing. He was married but now was single, he had one child. Because of coronavirus he was not dating anybody for the moment, however he was looking for a woman to share trips and photography.

René

René had contacted me early in September: "Hello, I am attracted to you, but I am not an expert in online dating sites. Would you like to see me for a tea in the afternoon? With kind regards, René."

I sent back: "Hello René, excuse me, I have not looked at the site for many days, but yes it would be my pleasure to meet you."

After our first meeting, René wrote: "Thank you for the meeting, it is too early to know, if there was something. Maybe you have already decided 'NO' with your heart. I hope for a friendship, if possible. Greetings, René."

René: "I am too old to make a mistake. Young people can do so but at my age, the next woman I meet, I want to marry, and there should not be a failure. In Luxembourg, it is easy to meet when you are young but there are no older people here. In addition, I am looking for somebody with education, with culture and there are no such people here. Especially in the banks, most bank employees are highly paid, scandalously highly paid, without ever having a particle of brains. Most of the people here in Luxembourg have no education at all. They are dull. Highly paid but dull. I am looking for a woman with a certain level of education. It will be easier to find such a woman in Paris, the choice is bigger in Paris. Luxembourg is too small, the choice is too small."

René: "My wife passed away last year in August, she had breast cancer. Yes, I am crying about her death every day.

We were married for nearly forty years. She suffered a lot when I became unemployed the first time in 2009, after the financial crisis of 2008-2009, she just didn't stand the fact that I lost my job. It was very difficult for her. Now, she has been dead for a year. I cannot stay alone the rest of my life, therefore I enrolled on several online platforms, without being very active. To tell you, you are my first ever contact on Meetyourlove. I am not much used to these kind of meetings. I'll start giving away her clothes and things, it makes no sense keeping all her belongings and to be reminded all the time of her missing so much. It is not simple to be a widower, however I want to look into the future. With coronavirus it is difficult to meet a woman."

Jordan

"You know," I wrote to Jordan, "we should contact Carl's son, to talk with him and see if we could talk any sense into his father. He should take action in one direction or the other, but his wife needs to be informed about him having this relationship with me. What do you think?"

Jordan: "You are right, we should go talk with Carl's son one day. Whenever you are ready."

Carl

"How is your hand? Better?"

Carl: "I prefer to stay at home. My hand hurts. I cannot go cycling."

TIME FOR A TALK

She should know

Bernard

"There is only one explanation: His wife has found out about your relationship and she has been 'frying' him since. C has arrived at a fork in the road: he needed to make a decision whether he should walk left or right and he has decided to keep his family intact. This is the end of the line for your relationship.

Sorry, but it was expected... the only question was how long it was going to take...."

Carl

I prepared my next encounter with Carl. What was I going to tell him?!

"Since we first met, you have shown me beautiful Luxembourg by bike.

Since the lockdown, we cycled over 5000 kilometres together.

However, even with all these positive moments and experiences, there are even more negative feelings. You are capable of dropping me like a hot potato, just to save your own skin.

You will never leave your wife. This was the first sentence you told me and you repeat it often enough. I am always reminded of what my position is, the mistress, the other woman.

The day you hurt your hand, I must say I was humiliated by your ability to let me drop, to ignore me, to push me away, just because you had no more excuses to get out of your house. 'I prefer to stay at home'. When I read this sentence, it became very clear to me where our relationship stands.

There is one other point that intrigued me, still does.

May I ask why you never read the books I gave you? Why did you just put them away, without ever opening them even once?

Why?

Are you not curious?

Do you already know the content – or at least you think you know the content?

Are you so arrogant?

Why? I really don't understand.

I think I deserve better.

This is the end of our relationship."

There was the first real rain for a long time. In Florida and in the Caribbean, there were five hurricanes in a row. All of the objectives of the World Forum on Climate Change in 2010 were NOT met. All of them. Not one single objective achieved, yes, all of them failed. This means the earth heating up, water scarcity, refugees, problems with migration and rising sea levels.

Wednesday, 16 September 2020

Harry had his online session on networking and I told him about my book. He said, "In your next book, I'll be Romeo Winterland!"

Bernard

"Like any other self-centred man I can testify that the less a woman wants a man the more that man wants the woman. It is the rule of scarcity. The less something is available the higher the price we are willing to pay for it.

Your man is in trouble. He has to explain to his wife where and with whom he is spending his time. Every time he returns home his wife asks him: 'Did you see her today?' and then he has to lie...

Just skip it... there are so many others available.... you should find a cyclist who is young and unmarried..."

Thursday, 17 September 2020

In the evening, while teaching Luxembourgish to a witty, young lady who also wanted to sign up to Meetyourlove, I contacted a certain Samuel giving him my phone number. He replied: "You are fast, that's what you mean with 'speedy', now how about topping that and meeting at Café de Paris?"

We met there and spoke but I went home with a negative feeling. This man was so jealous he would never be able to be my partner. He was the typical teacher type of man, very ignorant despite his studies, he didn't know anything about subjects and topics outside his speciality. That was depressing.

Carl

Carl had written me a message: "Please Julia, let me know at least if you are in good health?"

I didn't reply.

I thought, "He will have to come to see me and then I'll ask him to take a decision. Stay with his wife or leave his wife. If he decides to stay with his wife, then it is over for good." I was convinced that he would stay with his wife. So that would be the end of it. However there was a small possibility, just a very tiny possibility that Carl would leave his wife. Therefore, I would need to stay strong and wait. No messages, no phone calls. Nothing. Just wait and see what happens and see what he decides. It was his decision.

Alan

"You should be firm with Carl. If you really want him to leave his wife, then you have to tell him this and set an ultimatum. You will not see him as long as he doesn't talk to his wife to clarify the situation. However you have to know that, even if he tells her, what kind of wife will accept living under the same roof with her husband who cheats on her? After all of this, he will not be the same.

The fun times you are having now are definitely over, he will be another man after this. Even if he saves his money and house. He will not be the same after. He didn't read the book. He would have been very upset because you have seen all those different men from Meetyourlove. I would have been very upset and jealous knowing that you met all of those men.

If you really love him, then be firm, don't write, don't call him, don't get weak, but wait until he comes to see you to talk to you and then you tell him to leave his wife, or that's the end of it. There is a big chance that he will say, that's the end. Maybe not. Some women hope this, some succeed, some don't. Only time will tell. However, if you presented yourself to his wife to talk to her, to tell her about your affair with her husband, this would immediately mean the end of your relationship."

Saturday, 19 September 2020

The Tour du Luxembourg bicycle race had been running for a few days and the finish was on Saturday in Limpertsberg, where I went to meet friends. There was finally a real social gathering after such a long period of lockdown.

Sunday, 20 September 2020

Louis re-started his Sunday Fitness classes with over a hundred participants.

I was waiting for Carl to come to see me. I knew he would be coming one day. Until then I would have to be patient. He needed to talk with his wife to clarify the situation. I didn't want to meet any other men on the website. I would be going biking today, alone, in the Red Rock area, as it was going to be one of the last warm and sunny days. Summer was really over.

More than 18000 new infections in one single day in France.

More than 2000 new infections in a single day in Germany.

In Luxembourg, more than 180 new cases in one day.

There is talk of a second wave of coronavirus in Europe.

However, the Luxembourg government decided there would be no second lockdown. The economy could not stand it. They asked everybody to wear their masks and to socially distance.

A friend told me, "In France, they do not wear their masks and they don't keep their distances. That's why the numbers of infections are rising. The restaurants are packed, as before, as if there were no coronavirus. The metro in Paris works like before, everybody stuck in there, squeezed in there. In Marseille, they party, young people party, old people party, everybody parties and so on."

Saturday, 26 September 2020

Carl

Of course, he finished with his bad mood, and met me on Tuesday. We enjoyed our walk in the forest. It was dry and sunny and the trees were colourful. We watched the sunset at our favourite spot, on top of the world with a view.

The week continued with a lot of work, teaching classes online, and biking with Carl in the afternoon, while the weather changed from thirty to eight degrees within just one day.

Carl wrote:

"I wish you good luck with the webinars."

"I am going grocery shopping then we are going biking."

So far, I had asked Carl every day if he had read my book, or if he had read the article about it. So far, he said he hadn't.

More contacts

I was contacted by various men on Meetyourlove, among them a certain Armand, who said he liked the fact that I also travel and go skiing. Another one, Bruno, said he would regain his physical appearance with me as his personal coach. Pierre wrote he wanted to phone me and get to know me better. Xavier said he liked my profile on the platform, especially the photos. Rainier liked my smile and wanted to meet me when he was next in Luxembourg.

Then Marlon phoned to tell me, "I met a woman from Meetyourlove in person. She was already quite old and was good looking, quite younger looking. However, she was so afraid of coronavirus, she didn't want to go eat and drink, she was afraid of touching and so this put an end to the encounter. If you cannot be a bit closer to someone, this is no fun."

MEETING YOUR LOVE

For some reason, the number 27 always brings me luck.

Sunday, 27 September 2020

Louis taught his last fitness class on Facebook on Sunday morning. This class had been happening since the start of the lockdown. He even had a newspaper article published about it. I attended most of his Sunday mornings.

After an entire Saturday spent on the dating platform, on Sunday I continued checking my messages. There was Pascal, a teacher with two adult children, he liked biking and movies and walking and swimming and music and wanted to know me better. He wanted to meet me that same afternoon in Metz. He was really pushy, called several times in a row and asked so many questions, and wrote so many messages. This was too fast for me and I declined the meeting.

And returned to the platform to continue looking.

There was a sporty one, Gérard, on his bike, I wrote him a message, he replied: "Besides your nice looks, we have a lot in common, call me!"

I went jogging while calling him. He told me his story, I told mine. We were both sporty but the only thing was he lived quite far away. So we continued writing and phoning over the next days and weeks without ever meeting in person. Gérard always said: "You are always welcome to come and see me!" The distance prevented this meeting in person.

I continued searching on the platform. There was a Christian, who worked just around the corner from my place, but lived a bit far away, who was definitely too young and not much interested in me. He preferred going out with his friends to eat and drink, despite coronavirus. He never called nor wrote back. I thought, "He is not interested, that's all."

The next one I contacted was Douglas.

"How are you with this weather? Hope to read you soon," I wrote.

He replied, "Hello, thank you for your message, yes, I am fine, I am away for the weekend, but the weather is bad here too."

We continued writing on the platform, then exchanged phone numbers and continued the conversation on WhatsApp.

Douglas: "Afternoon."

"Hello, nice to see you here," I replied.

Douglas: I sent you some pictures from today.

Douglas: I have to be on the road now. I am happy to be in contact with you. Talk to you later. I hope...

"Me too, am happy to talk to you. Wishing you good driving. You pay attention on the road, it is raining and the streets are slippery. We can talk later, if you wish. I will exercise now."

Douglas: "Yes, of course, we can talk later, with pleasure. Have a good time at sports."

Douglas's profile said: "I want to meet a dynamic and sympathetic person. People say that I am generous and kind. I like going away for weekends, laughing, having a good time. Love is an extraordinary feeling, it allows you to project yourself and to be much more optimistic, relaxed, well in your body and your head...If I had one hour free, I would do some sports, enjoy evenings with my friends, some nice weekends, hiking, movies, cultural events..."

On that same Sunday afternoon, while I was jogging in the Pétrusse valley, I came across Samuel, who was there for a walk. We continued together. "You are good looking," he said, "but you are not free! I do not want a woman who is not free."

"Well, you know, I am on Meetyourlove to meet somebody because my current boyfriend is married and I cannot live with this situation. It's unbearable."

"No, I'll not give you my phone number, I am hesitant, you might follow me, no, it is better like this."

"We could start by being friends."

"I don't know, no, really, I prefer not," Samuel said. "Well," I thought, "it's better that I won't see him again, because he is way too complicated in his head."

A little later that evening, Jordan called and asked, "Julia, are you at home? I'll come over and give you a present."

Jordan came by and gave me a bottle of fruit juice. He stayed 10 minutes in front of the door and left with his mask on.

Douglas

Douglas wrote the following day: "Hello, how are you?"

"I am fine, thank you."

Douglas: "I wish you a nice day. I am happy to be in contact with you."

"Me too. I am teaching a language class now, I'll write to you later, if you wish."

Douglas: "Enjoy your class, we can talk later, with pleasure."

...

I asked him many questions. "Hello Douglas, what do you for work? Do you also speak Luxembourgish? And German?"

Douglas asked her, "Have you been single for a long time?"

"Do you think we could meet to discuss these private things, I don't like writing about them."

A little later in the day.

"Douglas, what is your family name please?" I asked him, "And is Douglas your real name?"

Douglas: "It's a pseudo."

"I have gotten used to Douglas, may I still call you Douglas?"

"Yes of course, it's a nice name."

"I found you on the internet. Have a look at this link, is that you?"

"Yes, that's me."

"But it says you are older than you say you are on Meetyourlove."

"I am not a specialist with online dating, well, yes, I am older than that."

"I have to go now, I'm teaching."

"Ok, until later… Julia, … is that your real name?" he asked.

Tuesday, 29 September 2020

Carl and I went mountain biking in Dudelange all afternoon. It had rained in the morning but had stopped and the afternoon stayed dry and warm. We did twenty kilometres through the forest, enjoying ourselves and the outdoors.

"What shall I tell Douglas now?" I thought after the bike ride with Carl, "This is not good, it is not okay to meet him while being involved with Carl. Somehow, I have to figure out an excuse not to meet him. Or shall I still meet with him? But no, that's not fair, that's really not me."

After some more reflection in the evening, I wrote to Douglas: "Good evening Douglas, unfortunately I'll have to cancel our meeting tomorrow, Wednesday. In fact, I am looking for a younger man. With my apologies."

Douglas: "Oh, well, I understand, but are you sure?"

"Please let me think some more. I'll tell you later."

Sometime later, Douglas wrote: "I think it is better to cancel our meeting."

Carl

On Friday, Carl and I met again at the cemetery in Schifflange to go mountain biking. The next day the sports program would start again and I would have less free time for biking.

By now, Carl and I had cycled over five thousand six hundred kilometres together.

"This has been the most extraordinary summer in my life," observed Carl.

"Me too," I agreed, "This was so special, it really was. We have enjoyed ourselves so much. We discussed so many topics and solved the world's problems. By the way, did you read the book I gave you?"

"No, not yet. It is among the other books I still have to read. I even took it with me on my last holiday but there was no time for reading."

"How has your day been so far?"

"All morning my wife was arguing with me. She wants a divorce. She is so upset. She says that she wants to divorce but I don't want to because she will be poor, and me too. She says I'm away every afternoon for hours, without her knowing where I go to."

"Why don't you tell her that you have a girlfriend but that it would be best for everybody if she stays living together with you in the same house."

"No, I won't tell her. I know that she would not want that. And now, please, let's stop this discussion, I feel like I'm getting angry."

We continued biking and took some photos. The sun came out and, on our way back, we stopped at the lookout over Belval, where we sat down as always to enjoy the view. We ate some grapes, cheese and bread with water from the bike bottles. After a while, we returned back home.

"Have a nice evening, Carl."

"You too, Julia. It really was the most extraordinary summer ever!"

Back home, I knew that Carl would have other discussions with his wife asking for a divorce and him refusing it.

I sat at my computer to work. After finishing and having prepared my classes for the next day, I had a look at Meetyourlove, and after some thought decided to follow the general trend and make a few changes to my profile. First, change my name, nobody was there with their real names. Second, change my photos and add some more interesting ones.

Thursday, 1 October 2020

Patricia: "So, did your changes on Meetyourlove impact your success rate?"

"Patricia, you won't believe me," I answered, "but now, after having changed my name and the pictures, there are many more contacts, yes, even more men contacting me and writing to me. But some of them have such horrible photos, incredible, a cabinet of horrors. And old. No, I'll never go out with any of those."

Patricia: "So Carl's wife wants the divorce?"

"Yes, I'll just sit back and wait. His wife will do it all alone."

"That's the best strategy. And never put any pressure on him. On the contrary, be on the defensive and wait for him to come to you."

"Thank you for your advice. In the meantime, I'll continue on Meetyourlove."

"Maybe there'll be a rare pearl in the horror cabinet, ha!"

There were several contacts on Meetyourlove. Rudolf, from Germany who didn't understand why he should talk in more than one language. He was sporty, a cyclist, but lived too far away and had bad knees. Then there was Walter, another cyclist, but not interested. I exchanged messages with Tim and Ralph and a few more who, on the whole, were seriously looking for a relationship. I thought about writing an academic publication about my research on the dating platform. Strangely, I found people to be unexpectedly honest. Yes, they lied about certain things, like their name for one, but they also shared their life stories and were more intimate and personal.

US President Donald Trump and his wife First Lady Melania tested both positive on coronavirus. Donald Trump was hospitalized, tweeting: I am fine, I hope. Love.
Other White House Members and Senate Members tested positive. They all had been attending an election campaign event, apparently without wearing masks and without social distancing.

Sunday, 4 October 2020

I spent some time on Meetyourlove, searching and reading men's profiles. Gustave wrote this about himself: "I am divorced. I like the pleasures of life as much as the discovery of the countryside, sports, tennis, ski, boating, golf.... Good wine and travel. Please upload your photos without sunglasses if you want a reply." Michael wrote: "I like your profile, maybe we could telephone, this would be nicer and meet in person, please give me your phone number."

Raphael wrote: "I am a cyclist too! Respect for your activities. Don't change anything! Please remain who you are, you are a beautiful young woman. Hope to read you soon, I would be happy to talk to you. No cycling with this weather."

We exchanged phone numbers and called. We talked and talked. Unfortunately, Raphael lived far away, and worked night shifts. He had no way to meet me in person, as he worked at night and during the day slept or went for bike rides.

Raphael: "I am so unhappy, because I really like you, I would have liked to have a woman like you. You are with this married man, he doesn't deserve you. He should decide. Either he is with you or he is with his wife. But he cannot have both. You should stop going out with him. I would like to have a woman like you, you are exactly my type of woman, funny, sporty, young, full of energy and very beautiful."

I wrote back: "I am so unhappy. You are right, I should take a decision and leave this married man with his wife."

Raphael: "He doesn't really love you. He only takes advantage of you. He spends good times with you, and then goes back to his wife, kids, house, car, dog etc. He has it all. Why should he change?"

"You are right."

"You should be looking for a new boyfriend, someone who is available and who is a cyclist. A man just for you. One day you will meet such a man if you want to."

"What do you recommend I should do?"

"You could talk with your married man, or with his wife, or with his kids, and then see what happens. He should take a decision and if he doesn't, you could provoke it. I am going for a bike ride now, bye."

"You really think so?"

In the following days Carl and I met up twice.

I continued exploring Meetyourlove. I was contacted by Alano, a cyclist and mountain biker, but he lived too far away. His kids worked in Luxembourg but he lived in a little village far away. "What a pity, they all live far away," I thought to myself.

Bars and pubs were closed in Paris but not restaurants.

Brussels also decided to close all bars and pubs. And there was no more drinking alcohol outdoors.

Over 4000 new infections in Germany in one day.

Over 18000 new infections in France in a day.

Over 140 new infections in Luxembourg in a day.

They were saying that the coronavirus had mutated.

US President Donald Trump returned after only three days of hospitalization to the White House and continued his election campaigning despite his coronavirus infection.

Thursday, 8 October 2020

Jasmine told me about her mother in the care home. The coronavirus had entered the home and many elderly people were infected, Jasmine's mother included. She was isolated in her room and so Jasmine couldn't visit her. It was only possible to telephone from time to time but this was difficult. These are really trying times for everybody.

Jordan

On Thursday afternoon, Jordan and I had our badminton class. In coronavirus times, social distancing rules and mask wearing even applied to the indoor classes.

After the game Jordan said, "Julia, I have a surprise for you. I shouldn't tell you. But the surprise arrived today. By parcel. From Canada."

"What is it? Tell me, I am curious!"

"My wife knitted a red wool scarf for you for Christmas from her own sheep. Yes, the wool is from her sheep in her garden. It's red, because I told her that your favourite colour is red!"

"Oh, what a wonderful surprise, a red scarf, knitted by your wife especially for me! This is absolutely fantastic!"

"Please put the pictures of today's Badminton class on your Facebook, so that everybody can see it!"

Tuesday, 13 October 2020

Carl

Carl: "Where are you, Julia?"

"I am on my bike, coming back from a sports class, I'm going uphill, out of breath."

Carl: "Can we go ice skating?"

"Yes, with pleasure!"

Carl: "See you then."

We met for the ice skating class at Kockelscheuer.

There were twelve people in the skating class and the coach was very professional.

Carl and I stayed a while after the class to practice what we had just learned.

There were 6300 new infections in one day in Germany.
In France, there was another partial lockdown again: from nine at night to six in the morning.
In Germany, there was a partial lockdown in certain towns and bars, pubs and restaurants had to be closed again.

Thursday, 15 October 2020

Gérard had a bike accident! So far, we had known each other via Meetyourlove but had phoned and written from time to time. He wrote from the hospital in Thionville that he had broken his hips and femur. From this day on, we phoned and wrote more often.

Gérard told her, "It will need a lot of patience and hard work to get back to normal."

"Never give up!" I encouraged him, "And remember you are on Meetyourlove to find a partner and one day you will find the right woman."

Gérard said, "Thanks. And you, I think you should stop wasting your time on this married man and look for a free man. I would have been interested in you, but now with this accident I am somewhat out of the game, sorry. Why don't you stop this absurd relationship, or why don't you clarify the situation with him? Or with his wife, or his kids?"

"Ah, I maybe could go talk to his wife, or his children."

"A crazy but efficient idea," agreed Gérard.

All carnival events were cancelled. There were more than 7000 infections in one single day in Germany France introduced a coronavirus curfew.

Friday, 16 October 2020

"Gérard, how are you today?" I wrote.

Gérard: "You are an early morning bird today! My pain is slowing down... Do you have time for a chat?"

"So how's it going then, in the hospital?"

Gérard: "Well, I realise how good it was to walk, to run and to go bike riding I want you to be my nurse and you can come cure me here and also at home. Like every man, I fantasise about such a thing. Now, I have a broken hip and cannot walk even from my bed to the door. Now, I am a broken man, but I'll look to the future and be positive. It is about resilience. If Carl didn't read your book, I don't know what to do to make him read it. As soon as I am out of here, I'll give you my address and you come to see me."

"How can I make Carl read my book and how to make him leave his wife?"

"You could post a book to his wife, best send it from France, in an envelope with French stamps on it. Or send it to his daughter, or his son. This would be an atomic bomb."

"Well, I would not do it, because I never harm anybody. But he would read it after his wife had hit him on the head with it!"

"At least we'd have a good laugh."

Saturday, 17 October 2020

The Luxembourg government met in a special committee to decide about further measures to combat the pandemic. After many delays throughout the afternoon and evening the Prime Minister finally announced, "We will not take further measures."

I had been nervous and anxious for the last few days. France had decided to have a curfew. Not everywhere, but in coronavirus hotspots like Strasbourg, where there were huge traffic jams on the bridge from Strasbourg to Kehl, with French people stocking up on everything useful and eventually almost emptying the neighbouring supermarkets in Germany.

So, there was at least some good news in Luxembourg.

But financially and economically this was a catastrophe. Nobody talked about the suicides that occurred because people did not see any financial solutions. Restaurants, bars, pubs, travel agencies and flight companies were all heavily affected.

Economically this could have unknown impacts, with worldwide shutdowns, loss of work and falls in real estate prices. People would stop paying rent, or worse may have no money for food, while a few companies made huge profits.

In the fitness class, Jordan helped me to keep up my spirits.

Jordan said, "You are too pessimistic, Julia, don't be so pessimistic. You remember when you told me that after the lockdown people would not come back to the sports classes, and now you have even more people than before. Don't worry. I love you."

After the sports class, I had my German lesson with Stefano, my favourite student. We were reading Emanuele Coccia's Die Wurzeln der Welt. Eine Philosophie der Planzen, Stefano's favourite book.

There was again a problem with the phone line and the Internet connection. What a disaster. Because of the street works, the construction of the tram line and a hotel just in front of my house, this had been happening regularly. What's more, my computer decided to do a general update, with several shutdowns and restarts lasting about an hour.

When there are so many things going wrong at the same time, the body switches to self-protection mode.

Carl hadn't answered my messages, but eventually we agreed to go riding in the afternoon in the Red Rock area. That was typical of him, not to answer messages directly but to make people wait.

Carl

Schifflange cemetery. An odd place to meet.

It was a grey day, no rain but some sunshine and cold.

While taking some pictures of the colourful, autumnal leaves in the forest, I asked Carl, "Did you have a look at my book yet?"

"No."

"Ah, okay."

Later during our bike ride, I asked again if he had looked at the book?

"No, nobody will steal it."

"Aren't you a bit curious about what is written in it?"

"Hmmmm...."

"Where do you keep the two books I gave you?"

"I put them on the table in the living room."

"Both books?"

"Yes, both books. Nobody is interested in what I put there."

"Ah, okay."

"When the winter comes and with the colder weather, maybe..."

I didn't say anything else on the subject. I had a big silent laugh and later told my mother. She said, "It's so funny. It's been two months and every day ever since I've asked him about it in different ways and he still doesn't realise anything. It's funny. Especially with my book lying on their living room table. I mean, if his daughter reads it, she would say 'Daddy, this could be you in the book.' But well, we'll see what happens. I will not tell him that I wrote it. He has to find out by himself."

My mother laughed and said, "This is better than a comedy!"

"Yes. Sometimes Carl gets upset about me asking him about it all the time. Jasmine took one second to realize I was the author. Alan read it in one go after he got it. While Carl does nothing."

"It's because he just can't imagine that you could be the author. He thinks it's another unimportant paperback. He can't imagine that he is part of this book or even that he is the protagonist of it."

Monday, 19 October 2020

On Meetyourlove, I was contacted by Johan, sporty and kind but also living too far away.

Alan

Alan on the phone with me: "I am so angry!"
"Why are you angry?"
"I am angry. Because you stay with this married man."
"Oh!"
"It was all a mistake."

Jordan

"Luckily you are in good health, my dear Julia. Please always remember that I'll never leave you when you are in need."

Tuesday, 20 October 2020

Carl

I went biking with Carl in the Red Rock area. The weather was sunny and it was turning out to be a golden autumn.

"What was the last book you read?" I asked him.

"The last book I read was by Ranga Yogeshwar, the physicist. You know, I'm never at home, well a bit in the morning, but every afternoon I am with you. Nearly every day. When the winter comes, maybe I'll have more inspiration to read."

---

417 new coronavirus infections in one single day in Luxembourg.
Ireland shuts down for a second complete lockdown.

Thursday, 22 October 2020

I had a rehearsal for my university webinars. The next one was on Monday with over a thousand people already enrolled.

I also taught online German and Luxembourgish classes and a senior's badminton class.

All day it was unusually warm for the season.

Carl wrote, he was suffering from a migraine all day long without feeling better, not even in the evening.

Friday, 23 October 2020

Carl was still ill, he wrote.

Louis

I called Louis, my fitness instructor colleague and good friend whom I had convinced to join Meetyourlove and asked, "How is it going?"

"Oh, we have to meet in person," Louis answered, "Are you free Sunday? We'll have a drink together. So many things have happened. I have met so many people, had so many stories."

"Me too, I even wrote a book about it!" I informed him.

"Really? Please I need to read it! Bring it along on Sunday!"

"But it has to stay confidential."

"Of course. This is private. Now, for me, all this process has been therapeutic."

"Let's write the next book together, or I'll write my second book and you also write your book about dating in Coronavirus times."

"That's a fantastic idea! You know, I have kept notes of all of my meetings with all of these women, so it'll be possible to retrace everything and to write a book about it!"

"Excellent!"

"We'll see each other on Sunday, and then we talk about all of this. Bring your book with you for me. I absolutely need to read it!"

Raphael

The same Friday, Raphael wrote: "I just came back from a bike ride. How are you, beautiful lady? And how is it going with your dear married boyfriend? You shouldn't waste your time with a married man who only takes advantage of you. Get rid of him and get a new one. I would like to have a woman like you but you live too far away. One day, maybe we'll meet in person and then we will see if we have any feelings for each other. But don't stay with this one. You are wasting your time and energy."

"Well, you're right, Raphael, it's so frustrating," I agreed, "At the moment he is sick and he's staying home with his wife so I can't see or phone him. This waiting for his messages drives me crazy."

Raphael: "Don't wait for his messages! You will find another man and soon. I would be happy to have a woman like you. Please listen to me and get yourself a proper boyfriend. I'll keep biking and working at nights and won't have many chances to meet nice women but you have the chance to meet nice men! Your heart is filled with a man who doesn't deserve you. Get rid of him! Soon!"

And Raphael continued: "Either he divorces his wife and gets together with you or this cannot continue. That's my point of view but you have to see it for yourself."

I told him, "I'll inform his wife."

"That's a bit dangerous! He'll never forgive you."

"So, what should I do?"

"It's up to him to decide."

"He's already made a choice. He'll never leave his wife. Therefore, I go on with my life. But I have to inform his wife. She has to know. Or another person has to tell his wife. She needs to know!"

Raphael replied, "Yes, you're right, maybe he will not be happy but you need to do it. This is the danger of being with a married man."

Over 45000 new infections in coronavirus in France in one day, despite the curfew.
Over 10000 new infections in coronavirus in Germany in a day.
Over 900 new infections in Luxembourg in one day.
The Government announces new measures.

Saturday, 24 October 2020

Jordan, Alan

Jordan and I went together to Saarbrücken, to meet friends, being careful to socially distance and wear masks.

During dinner Alan called and said, "Yes, I am angry, because you are staying with this married man who will never leave his wife. This really makes me really angry. You have to tell him to leave his wife."

"His wife has to know," I said.

"It has to be him to leave his wife," Alan insisted, "He has to take the decision. Not her. He has to stand behind you."

Jordan, overhearing this, said, "Julia, I'll help you, we will tell his wife. She has to at least sense what her husband is doing. You know how his wife must feel. She thinks there is something going on. She asks him if he's lying. If he's lying like this with her, one day he'll be lying to you. Be careful."

HOMEWRECKER, DESTROYER OF WORLDS

Sunday, 25 October 2020

Louis invited me for dinner to talk about his experiences with meeting women on Meetyourlove. Despite some promising starts, he was still alone and still searching. As bizarre as some encounters were, he hadn't lost hope.

Regarding Carl, Louis was clear. He said, "Your idea to go talk to his son is maybe not the best, but better than nothing. In my opinion, Carl doesn't love you, regardless of what he says. He is only taking advantage of you. It's an idea to go tell his wife. However, it might be better to tell his son first. What do you have to lose? But don't go alone, make sure Jordan goes with you."

Jordan

"I'll help you, Julia. I'll go to talk to Carl's wife, while you are out with him. She has to know."

Louis

"I have bought a new car, a red Ferrari! This has always been my dream. I bought it second hand and for one month I was negotiating the price. I'll get it this week. My ex-girlfriend said she wants to be the first woman to go for a ride with the new Ferrari, otherwise she doesn't want to go for a ride at all!"

Monday, 26 October 2020

Patricia and I talked over Skype every day. Because of the new restrictions, people were increasingly isolated.

Patricia said, "Hopefully they will not close the borders again. That way you could come to visit on Sunday!"

"They cancelled my sports classes for tomorrow morning, so you never know what they are capable of deciding. People all over the world are protesting against the measures. People are having financial problems. Why should they close their restaurants? What for? This makes no sense. We need social contacts."

Later in the day, I called Jordan and asked him, "Could you come this evening after my last sports class to see Carl's son Brian and to talk to him, please?"

Jordan replied, "I thought our plan was that I go talk to Carl's wife tomorrow, while you go ice skating with him, but if you think it is better to talk to his son, then yes. Brian will certainly be with his girlfriend, so he won't feel outnumbered."

...

After the lesson, Jordan was waiting in his car outside. The following week, there would be no sports as all the classes had been cancelled.

Jordan asked, "Are you nervous?"

"No. You drive here right and then left and then-"

"Yes, thank you, I know the street where Brian lives,.... And here we are, let's park here, just in front of the house."

"Good, let's ring the bell."

"Well, no reply. Let's ring all the bells," suggested Jordan, "Somebody will open the entrance door."

Jordan and I went up the stairs to the second floor and knocked at the door. We tried other doors but had no luck. It was getting late. We went back to the foyer and tried the intercom again. This time it was answered by a shy female voice.

Jordan: "Oh, hello, finally, we were about to give it up. Can we talk to Brian please?"

Brian's girlfriend: "Brian is here, but who are you?"

Jordan: "I'm Jordan and I'm with Julia."

Brian's girlfriend: "Brian says he doesn't know any Jordan or Julia."

Jordan: "That's true, that's the reason why we are here."

Me: "We want to introduce ourselves."

Brian: "I'll not open the door or let you in. It's late and dark, I don't know you."

Me: "That's exactly the reason why we want to talk to you."

Brian: "Why, I don't understand. What do you want?"

Jordan: "This is a family matter, we want to talk about your family."

Brian: "I don't know you and I have no family business to discuss with you."

Jordan: "Could we come back another day and time?"

I was getting desperate and said, "I'm very sorry that it's so late but I teach in the evening. Please, we would like to talk with you but it's a delicate matter and not to be discussed over an intercom."

Brian: "No, I am not going to let you in. Please, no."

Jordan: "Okay... We are here to tell you that my friend here is the girlfriend of your father."

Brian: "I don't want to be involved in this."

The door buzzer was buzzing loudly.

Jordan: "We don't want to discuss this like this but we came to talk to you. Maybe you could talk with your mother."

The door buzzer was buzzing so loudly, it was difficult to understand what he was saying.

Brian: "I don't want to be involved in this. This is my parents' problem, not mine. How did you get my address by the way?"

The door buzzer was buzzing even louder.

I suggested, "Maybe you could talk with your father then, if you don't want to involve your mother."

Brian: "Ah, come in please, you can come in."

Jordan to me: "We can come in!"

"Yes, we can come in!" I exclaimed.

The door buzzer continued.

We walked up the stairs where Brian welcomed us with a warm greeting. In his eyes I saw warmth, intelligence and curiosity. Brian stood and looked at me for a long time. We all were wearing masks, so it was difficult to read anything else other than the eyes.

Brian and his girlfriend invited us in, there were two cats on the living room table staring at us.

Brian's girlfriend stood in the kitchen and remained there all the time. Indeed, it was not her business.

Brian: "Do you want to drink something?"

"Yes, please," I said, "I've been teaching three hours of sports in a row. I'm thirsty."

Jordan: "Now, we are here to introduce ourselves out of respect for women. That is why we are here."

Brian: "Ah, so tell me please."

He looked curiously at me and I returned his look.

Jordan: "I have this wonderful friend here, who is a good friend of mine, and also an even better friend of your father, so we wanted to clear the situation because your mother should know this."

Brian: "I'm not going to tell my mother."

Jordan: "That's clear. This talking should be done by your father."

Brian: "I'm going to talk with Myriam, my sister."

I agreed with him: "That's a good idea. You talk this over with Myriam."

Brian: "I'll see what Myriam says, and..."

Jordan: "The two of you could talk with your father, to convince him to talk to your mother."

"I was not able to remain in hiding," I interrupted, "You know, if a relationship lasts a few months, then you don't say anything, but after a longer time, then something should be done. I can't stand this situation and see your mother suffer. Woman to woman, she needs to know."

Brian: "Why doesn't my father talk to my mother?"

"Because he is afraid of the financial ruin," I answered, "He doesn't want to sell the house. He doesn't want to divorce and he doesn't want to move out."

Brian: "My parents live their lives apart, they don't fit together any longer."

Jordan: "Life is too short to waste. You see, I have myself a wife and three children and..." He continued speaking about his life and his situation, and that he wanted to share his life with me "...and this includes my wife. She includes Julia in our family."

Jordan then spoke about his sports classes with Carl and me and they talked about the book, lying on the living room table at Carl's house.

Brian: "You're brave to come to talk to me. Thank you for coming and excuse me please for having been cold when you rang the bell."

"Excuse us for the late visit," I said.

So the evening went on. We kept our masks on, taking them off only for drinking our water.

It was getting late and I said, "Jordan, let's go home."

Jordan: "Brian, thank you for having talked to us. Thank you for your hospitality and your friendliness."

Brian: "I'll talk with Myriam and get back to you, maybe not tomorrow, but soon."

"Thank you and good night!"

Down in the street and back in the car, I turned to Jordan and said, "Thank you so much."

There were demonstrations in Italy against coronavirus measures.
In Germany, there were also demonstrations against new measures and regulations.

The day after, Carl and I went ice skating in the evening.

Carl said, "This is my first sports since I was sick last week and I'm still weak. But, imagine, my wife asked me before I left if I was going ice-skating. And then nothing! All the other times she made accusations that I had a girlfriend and so on, but this time, nothing."

I thought, "I think I know why."

France initiated a new lockdown starting Friday.
Bars, pubs, restaurants, cinemas and theatres were all to be closed.
Germany decided to have strict coronavirus regulations.

Wednesday, 28 October 2020

Bernard

My dear Julia,

I have to be sincere and straightforward with you.

The only reason for a woman to visit her lover's wife is to throw a hand grenade into an existing crisis and to create a situation where the man would leave his house. Moreover, to involve the children, even if they are already grown up, in the conflict is beyond my comprehension. The son has his own life and the last thing he needs is to get involved in his parents' disagreement. What do you expect him to do? And why him?

Your explanation that you wanted to put things in order by informing the wife about her husband's escapades is unacceptable. She already knows what she needs to know and it is not for you to get between husband and wife.

My hope is that the crisis in this family will explode and be sorted out by your pressure and that the man will decide to stay with his wife, for better or worse.

My reply to Bernard:

I knew that this would be your reaction.

I am so sorry to disappoint you so much.

Bernard's reply to me:

OK - your life, your call.

You have not disappointed me since you told me the truth. You were always truthful to me the same way you feel you need to be truthful to the wife. Sometimes being too direct (to the wife) does not help anyone (the same way you wouldn't tell a good friend her new dress is ugly).

Anyhow, I can preach as much as I want, the reality is that this is you, your life and your situation. I hope you achieve what you wanted in the first place, that Carl will stay at home and that his wife knows about you. Good luck.

My reply to Bernard:

We will see how it goes.

His son is a very kind, intelligent and well-educated young man. He said he was happy we came to talk. He said he will talk with his sister and they will see what to do.

Anyhow, I'll tell you what happens next.

Bernard's reply to me:

As ever, you are the most honest person I have met.

Love you.

As someone said, 'Have your love affairs two towns away from your own' :)

Luxembourg is too small to have undetected hanky panky...

Thursday, 29 October 2021

So far, there had been no reaction from the children, nor from Carl. Perhaps they had not spoken with their father yet. Perhaps they had and Carl was staying silent.

Carl

"I'll come to go for a walk."

Later, after our walk, I said, "Good night, sleep well." Carl replied, "You too."

Friday, 30 October 2020

All sports classes were cancelled. I decided to start up Distance Fitness again.

Carl and I went mountain biking again in the afternoon. Night fell early and before six it was dark in the forest.

So far, there had been no reaction from him.

I was anxious to know what Brian had decided to do. Had he talked with his sister yet? Had they talked with their mother?

Carl behaved as if nothing was different.

Jordan

"Do you have any news from Carl or from Brian?

It may take a couple of days for Carl and his wife to find the right way out."

Sean Connery passed away today, age 90. The James Bond par excellence.
On 3 November the US presidential elections will take place. Trump or Biden.

Saturday, 31 October 2020

Carl

With all sports classes being cancelled, I went mountain biking with Carl. As usual, we started from the cemetery in Schifflange. Many people were there to bring flowers to the graves of their loved ones for All Souls Day. This was a very different year as all graveside commemorations had been prohibited due to the coronavirus. People came individually, putting flowers and remaining in silence for a while.

We cycled in the forest, as usual.

Sunday, 1 November 2020

At seven in the morning, Jasmine, Jordan and I left for the three-hour drive to Germany to visit my mother, Patricia, for the day. It was a dark, rainy morning but still warm.

As we arrived at Patricia's house, we were greeted with joy and happiness. We went for a walk in the neighbourhood, with Jasmine looking at all the Halloween decorations in the gardens. The four of us had lunch together, a typical lunch with Maultaschen, a Schwäbisch speciality. Later, we had coffee and apple cake.

The drive back in the dark and with the rain was tiring but we really had enjoyed the day.

Monday, 2 November 2020

Tomorrow, would be the presidential elections in the USA. Donald Trump or Joe Biden. Donald Trump decided he would declare victory, even if he didn't win.

Carl

Carl and I went mountain biking, meeting again at Schifflange cemetery in the afternoon. It was warm and sunny when we left but a threatening sky with dark clouds came up. We chatted as usual during our bike ride.

"I like my family life with my kids," Carl told me, "but I also like to have a girlfriend, you. I like to have both."

"The secret of our love is that it is new every day," I said.

I decided that tomorrow, I would tell Carl that I had spoken to his son. I would tell him, "You want to have both: your wife, your kids, your house, your family and me. I have spoken with your son. And he has spoken with his sister. I suppose they already have spoken with your wife, their mother. That's why she is so quiet and relaxed."

And then I would see what he would say.

Distance Fitness back on again

Distance Fitness started again after only a one-month break. Tony, Peter and Jordan were especially keen of having the Distance Fitness class again. They were joined by Philippa, who had been ice skating with me. In our masks, we sweated and had fun. Loneliness was forgotten for a while.

Tuesday, 3 November 2020

Louis started up his twice-weekly fitness classes on Facebook again.

Carl

Carl and I met for our bike ride.

Carl said, "Just about a hundred kilometres more and I'll have done 9,000 kilometres this year."

"I'm up to 6,500. An absolute record!" I declared.

After the ride, back at the car, Carl said, "Julia, I love you so much."

"I love you too, Carl and I need to tell you that I have spoken with your son."

"What? When? You don't have his phone number."

"The week when you were sick. I went to speak with him."

Angrily, his eyes full of hate, he shouted: "If you really did this, then you talked with him about something that doesn't exist anymore. Don't you see how angry I am!? You abused my trust. Trust is built slowly over long time. You ruined everything in one second. I told you, I don't want my family to be involved. This is a complete no-go. I don't want this."

"Your son is an intelligent, friendly man. He likes me very much."

"It's over!" he shouted as he drove off angrily.

FRIENDS SAVE THE DAY

Wednesday, 4 November 2020

Carl

Furiously, Carl shouted at me on the phone: "You are so stupid, you ruined my happy family. What came to your mind to go and speak with my son! How dare you! I always said NO. You think you are so intelligent. You ruined a happy family! It is over! I'll stop the conversation now."

I shot back, "For me, it is unacceptable to go with a married man. It's been over a long time. You should have told your wife."

Bernard

My dear Julia

I assume you do not fully understand men. Men departmentalize their life and they may have one room assigned to the wife, one to the kids, one to the lover and one to the rest of the world. Men do not appreciate when those strict lines of separation between the various stakeholders get crossed.

Take it or leave it, but this is the reality and not what you have been trying to achieve by your calculated or miscalculated move. I guess you have known it all along and what you had tried to do was to send a message to Carl, everything or nothing. So you have got nothing.

Sorry about this development, I really want you to be happy.

Stay grounded and get on with your life. There is no other choice.

Kisses XXX

B

Thursday, 5 November 2020

Louis

"You did well to go to talk to his son and also to speak with Carl. Now you know that he doesn't love you.

There are several scenarios possible and this will take a while. Maybe he gets back happily with his wife and kids and they unite as a family. Or they separate or divorce. Or they continue the way they went on for all these years, him cheating on her.

This is a big opportunity for change and you did well to go talk to his son. You didn't ruin a happy family, you made them reflect on their situation and gave them the opportunity to change. Just wait and see, and if you need to talk, please call me, I'll always help you.

Don't despair! You had to do this, you couldn't continue the same way. It is good for a few months, but after a longer period, things in a relationship should move on, you cannot stay in hiding as his mistress for the next twenty years. Not you! And in a while, we will have a good laugh about the situation and how you went to talk with his son together with Jordan."

Distance Fitness in the dark

Distance Fitness took place in the dark. That was new. It had taken place in all weather conditions already, in the sun, in the heat, in the cold, in the rain and in the wind, but never in the dark before, so this was a novel, enjoyable experience. The lights from the balconies provided some light in the courtyard.

Friday, 6 November 2020

Louis

I messaged Louis: "Will you be teaching your Facebook Fitness on Sunday morning?"

Louis: "Yes, on Sunday, as usual. What are you doing tomorrow evening?"

"I am teaching but I'm free after that."

"Please come to my place. You and me and Philippa will have a pizza together. Better than staying all alone."

Saturday, 7 November 2020

In the evening, it was announced that Joe Biden would be the 46th President of the United States of America. This was a moment of joy and festivity for those who wished that Donald Trump would leave. It was unacceptable for Donald Trump and his supporters however.

I taught a German lesson with my favourite student and then went to Louis' place for the pizza. I found him with Philippa and her husband in his new red Ferrari.

We spent the evening together, laughing and enjoying good food and stories.

Philippa told me, "It must have been a shock for Carl and he overreacted. Let him digest the news. Now I understand why he was always so busy, he went cycling together with you. Don't do anything, go on with your normal life, see friends, enjoy your everyday activities, like drinking a good coffee or eating a good pasta. See friends and go out. Don't fall into depression, it is not worth it. Life goes on. Things will happen. You decided to make a move, he wanted to remain in his comfort zone for the next twenty years. I had a few affairs with married men before getting married myself, I know how it is to be sitting there and waiting for him to write or to call without ever being able to call. I fully understand your feelings."

When I got home that night I found a man on Meetyourlove whose handle was 'James Bond'. He didn't live in Luxembourg but came on business often. He suggested to meet the following Tuesday and go for a walk, 'because of coronavirus.'

A vaccine against coronavirus was discovered by Pfizer and BioNTech.
It would take some time to finalize it, but it seemed to work in 90% of cases.

Monday, 9 November 2020

A student of mine told me, "It's hell at my job. So many jobs are at risk because of coronavirus and I'm doing the work of other people and they still criticize my work. People are so aggressive because of coronavirus. It is unbelievable how horribly aggressive people are."

Tuesday, 10 November 2020

James

After teaching sports, I went for a walk with the James Bond from Meetyourlove who had first contacted me the previous week. The Autumn colours of the leaves were beautiful and we walked and talked.

"Please give me some time to build our friendship first," I requested, "I need time."

"Very good idea," said James Bond, "I am happy to see you. I'm ready to share my life with a woman again, it's not good being single all the time."

Wednesday, 11 November 2020

Apparently, today is the one hundredth birthday of James Bond.

James phoned me later that evening.

James said, "I wanted to tell you how much I enjoyed our walk yesterday and that I have been thinking about you."

"Thank you. I am still sad and I need time, time to heal and time to build up a friendship, if that's okay with you."

"Yes, of course. I'm eager to see you again. Next time, we could go to a restaurant."

"That'd be perfect."

Thursday, 12 November 2020

James wrote to me in the morning to wish me a nice day.

I was teaching my university and language classes online. I was enjoying my lessons so much and the students were amazing. One of the language students finished the entire beginner's book in only twenty lessons and was getting fluent!

There had been no news from Carl. I saw that he had unfriended and blocked me everywhere.

Distance Fitness took place in the evening in the dark and under the stars and a clear sky. Moving with the music it was not too cold. My students lingered afterwards to discuss politics and coronavirus restrictions.

Friday, 13 November 2020

Another Friday 13th of this year.

The first Friday 13th marked the lockdown in Luxembourg and it marked the resurrection of my relationship with Carl. That relationship was now definitely over.

Saturday, 14 November 2020

Tony called and told me, "I tested positive! I have coronavirus. A light fever, nothing serious. I'll have to quarantine for fourteen days. Obviously, I won't be coming to Distance Fitness."

I was in Saarbrücken when Tony called. All restaurants were closed because of the coronavirus. It was a strange town. There seemed to be so many sketchy people walking around or just standing. The Christmas tree was up but it had no lights and no decorations.

Mid November 2020

James. His name on MeetyourLove was James. James Bond. We exchanged several messages, phoned and met twice in person in mid-November 2020. James lived far away but worked in Luxembourg and I later thought all of this through, "James only contacted me, because I am living in Luxembourg City. As he lives far away, he thought it might be a good idea, having a girl, or different girls, where he could sleep overnight from time to time to save the money on hotels." He had told me that sometimes he got a hotel room to avoid driving all the way back and forth and he suggested sleeping at my place instead.

I remembered my response, "Oh no, there's not enough space in my apartment. It's too small."

I supposed that he had found many other women who agreed to have him overnight.

Not a bad idea this, sign up on Meetyourlove to have sex and lodging and dinner for free. Not a bad idea, just not a good one.

Saturday, 21 November 2020

I got a call from Tony who told her, "I am in hospital. I am not well with this coronavirus and am in hospital."

"Oh no, you have to get well soon. Promise!"

"Promise. There are not enough nurses here. I've been waiting for two hours."

In the early evening, I went for a lovely sunset walk with Beatrice, one of my friends. Because of the restrictions we couldn't meet indoors and so stayed outside.

Beatrice said, "It's so cold, I'll need a hot shower to unfreeze my bones. These talks with you are so great. I miss our discussions so much. This coronavirus shows all of us our real characters. It is so sad to hear how Carl behaved, how he let you down, as well as Alan, and now James. Unbelievable how people manipulate and take advantage of others. It's a reflection of our times."

Monday, 23 November 2020

At Distance Fitness, Jasmine brought a homemade cake for me saying, "This is for you. I made it for you, it's with apples and nuts. You'll love it!"

Jordan took part in shorts and a sleeveless shirt and Peter was in a t-shirt. It was getting chilly but as soon as you moved, you got warm.

Tuesday, 24 November 2020

I called Tony in hospital. "How are you?" I asked.

Tony replied with a weak voice, "Not good!"

"Please get well soon, we need you to come to Distance Fitness.

Tony's voice weakened even more, "Distance Fitness will have to wait, it will take a long time to recover."

Thursday, 26 November 2020

I spent the rest of the day on Meetyourlove reading messages from different men. I wrote to some of them.

I had two webinars and a language class to teach via Zoom. The webinars were very well attended.

In the evening, we had Distance Fitness and Peter and Jordan were again in their summer clothes while Jasmine was dressed warmly. The music and the dancing felt good.

LOVE IN TIMES OF…

Friday, 27 November 2020

Unbelievable but true: number 27, magical 27

Douglas

Just like most days now, I went on Meetyourlove to check for likes and messages.

It was a cold but sunny day in Luxembourg. I taught my online university classes and graded students' assignments in the morning. This was followed by German language classes. One student was new, it was his first German language class and he had never spoken German before in his life. He looked at me in astonishment when I said "Guten Morgen" to him.

To get some fresh air and relax, I went for a bike ride in the November sunset, however there were a lot of cars around as it was Friday afternoon.

The phone in my backpack rang, it was Alan, who said, "Hi Julia, ah, you are on your bike. I wanted to ask you for a bike ride at lunch, but I know you are teaching at lunch times, so I went alone. I drove to France to the hairdresser but everything is closed in France. This is not life. This is saddening. How long will the restaurants in France be closed for?"

"Until 15 January!"

"Oh, no, how will they survive without business over Christmas? They all will die, not from coronavirus but from hunger and financial problems. They don't earn much in normal circumstances. Where are we heading? Where?"

I rode back home and went for a quick walk in town when Jordan called: "You have to go to the city centre, there is this shop that has eighty percent reductions on everything. They have the most amazing mini-skirts that would fit you well. Or there's this jeans dress, all buttoned up in front, very sexy. Let me get it for you for Christmas! This would be the perfect gift for you from me. All these buttons in the front and you could leave some open..."

I finished my walk and returned home to my computer to go once again on Meetyourlove. There were some messages from a man in Germany who did not seem very interesting. He lived too far away and was too much of a civil servant, very boring despite the fact that he liked bicycling. His messages were all very flat. He seemed like the sort of person who criticised his colleagues for being boring and never changing but was worse than them.

I continued looking at who liked my profile and looking at their photos. "My God," I thought, "they all seem so old."

Just by chance I noticed that Douglas had visited my profile only a few minutes ago. We had been in contact on and off since September and had even talked on the phone and agreed to meet, but I had cancelled that meeting as I still was dating Carl. Now, with Carl gone for good, really for good, I thought, "Douglas is an interesting person, let's WhatsApp him."

I wrote to him: "Good evening Denis" (I even got his name wrong, oh no.) "Well, my profile is not going to get any better, even if you look at it more often :) How are you? What are you doing?"

Douglas: "Thank you for contacting me. I am fine, what about you?"

"Honestly, I have been working a lot lately. This situation of coronavirus has changed a lot our lives. Are you on your weekend now? Do you travel?"

Douglas: "Yes. I am on my week-end. I went to Italy this summer, and I spent a few weekends in the Vosges."

"Do you have a moment to talk on the phone or is it not possible to talk in person?"

Douglas: "You can call me. With pleasure."

Seconds later, I called him.

Douglas told me he was reading a book by Romain Gary called 'The Life Before Us', in Italian: 'La vita davanti a sé'.

I looked it up and found that Netflix had made the film of the book available just a few days previously. It starred Sophia Loren and her son Edoardo Ponti was the director. I spent the evening watching the trailer, listening to the title song 'Io sì' sung by Laura Pausini and watching various YouTube films about Sophia Loren, her life, her acting, her career, and her son and his work.

Douglas and I agreed to meet on Tuesday to see the Christmas lights in town. I said I was sorry for having cancelled the very first meeting back in September.

I remembered that I had said he was too old and Douglas had been very understanding and kind.

,gggg, ,hhh' Íhjkjj'

Sunday, 29 November 2020

Douglas surprised me today. We had been messaging earlier in the day and I had mentioned that I was going for a bike ride and then shopping.

Douglas: "Good morning. How are you?"

"What are you doing today?"

Douglas: "I am having lunch with my family today."

"Enjoy your lunch."

Douglas: "Thank you and what are you going to do?"

"I will go for a bike ride and then for shopping. Are you also going cycling?"

Douglas: "Yes, some mountain biking."

"If one day you have time we could go together."

Douglas: "Yes, of course, with pleasure."

"I love cycling."

Douglas: "You are very sporty. I am not as sporty as you."

"No worries."

Douglas: "I wish you a nice morning. Talk to you later."

He wrote back later and suggested he come shopping with me, so we would meet for the first time today instead of Tuesday.

Douglas: "What time are you going shopping?"

"Do you want to come with me?"

Douglas: "Yes. If you wish, that would be an opportunity to see each other."

"Very good idea. Around four would be okay for you?"

Douglas: "Yes, this will be okay. There will be a lot of people, I think."

"What kind of car do you have?"

Douglas: "Black"

"Perfect, I'll bearing wearing an anorak in the colours of the Luxembourg flag."

Douglas: "I will also put on an anorak, dark blue."

"And warm shoes!"

Douglas: "Yes."

It was a cold and cloudy day with little sunshine, but no rain or snow. Snow was forecast only in the coming days.

Douglas: "I will arrive in Luxembourg before four. This will allow us to enjoy some sunshine."

"You tell me when."

Douglas: "Three."

"That's good for me. I am home then."

Douglas: "Ok."

...

Douglas: "I just arrived. I am parking my car."

"There is a parking spot here."

Douglas: "I already found one."

We met in my street. I was waiting outside for Douglas. I looked up and down the street. I saw him walk towards me.

"He looks exactly as I had expected him to look," I thought. He looked at me curiously with his blue eyes. It was cold and we both were dressed in coats, hats, warm shoes and, of course, face masks. Despite all the coverings, a little bit of face and personality shone through. He looked at me curiously, tilting his head to study me better. "That's good," I thought, "he is a curious person who is interested in me."

We walked to the city centre, passing the 'Maison Streckeisen'. "Why is this house called 'Streckeisen'?" he asked curiously.

I replied, "Because it looks like an iron to iron your clothes."

"Yes, indeed, now I see it, thank you!"

"Do you want to go over or under the Adolphe Bridge?"

"Let's go under it, the bicycle path under the bridge is a masterpiece of construction."

In town, the shops were open but bars and restaurants were closed and had been for the last three weeks.

In France, Douglas needed to fill in a form saying that he is grocery shopping for essential needs.

We went for a walk in the Grund along the Pétrusse valley and the Alzette, taking in the Neumünster Abbey and the Wenzel Way, through the fortification walls to the bars and pubs and back to the Melusina monument where we took pictures.

Back in town, we went to the protestant church and attended the service. The congregation was dressed in their best clothes and in a multitude of colours.

From there we went to the catholic Cathedral to pray. In Grand Rue we managed to find a place with hot chocolate. Douglas and I went to the big heart on the Place d'Armes and wandered around looking at the decorations. It was soothing to see them. There were many people in town and it really was great just to watch them. Fortunately, it was not a dead town, at least today. There was life and activity despite the pandemic and all the lockdowns.

"You know," I said, "seeing all these decorations and lights, it would be super to go to Maastricht together, to see the lights there. The Christmas market there has been cancelled and to replace it they have also lights like in Luxembourg. They say they are really beautiful. And also in Bernkastel-Kues they will replace the Christmas market with lights. If you wish, we could go there as well."

"That's an excellent idea," agreed Douglas, "we could go together. But not tonight because I'll be visiting my mother at seven. Tonight she's making vegetable soup."

"Thank you for this nice afternoon together."

"Thank you. You are adorable. And, yes, you have a super idea: We will go to Maastricht together."

Tuesday, 1 December 2020 – Pétrusse

Douglas came to see me in the afternoon. We had messaged and spoken on the phone during the day. Even though it was raining, we walked for two hours through the Pétrusse valley and the city centre. Today, unlike Sunday, there was almost nobody in town, the wet streets were deserted. What an empty, depressing town this had somehow become. We went into St Michel's Church, where we lit a candle and admired the clock. Coming out of the church, we decided to have hot chocolate like we did on Sunday, but nobody was doing take out hot drinks today so I asked, "Would you like a tea at my place?" We were dripping with rain and cold and the tea and the cake were welcome. We continued our talk, it was an enjoyable afternoon and after Douglas had left, he wrote: "Thank you for the afternoon, I enjoy these moments with you."

Friday, 4 December 2020 – Saarbrücken

Douglas

Douglas: "Hello, Have a nice day Julia. I am thinking about you, all the time."

"Good morning. Hope you had a nice evening, my first lesson starts in 5 minutes :)"

Douglas: "Enjoy your lesson."

Douglas and I continued our Christmas lights tours and went to Saarbrücken. As like everywhere else, the Christmas market had been cancelled, but here at least there were a few well-spaced stands all over town and most places were lit with colourful lights.

"Shall we see some of the lights here?" Douglas asked me, "They put stars on the walls of the houses and lights on the ground. Look at this flat here. The windows are all lit in red. With the white facade, it certainly makes it stand out. Shall we have something to eat? There are some restaurants open for take away and we saw a few food stands also."

"Excellent idea. Let's go for some typical Saarländer specialities. How about a 'Schwenker'?

We went to get the 'Schwenker'.

"Let's sit down here on the benches," suggested Douglas, "It's not too cold."

"So tell me about your experiences with women on Meetyourlove," I wanted to know, "You told me you had seen two women before me, what happened? Why didn't it work out?"

"There is nothing really exciting about it. The first woman I met twice and we went to a restaurant and that's it. She had several problems. First, she was afraid of coronavirus and of the health of her mother and her own, and second, she was worried about her work, of losing her job. That was it. We didn't write again. I met the second woman in Arlon in a restaurant. We talked and after the meeting we wrote some more messages and then she didn't reply anymore. That was it."

"Yes, it's funny how things work out with other people. A man told me he had met a woman on Meetyourlove and they agreed to meet in person for a walk. She arrived in her car, he was waiting for her in the street, she opened the door of her car and stepped out of it in high heels. In high heels! They walked for about a hundred metres and then she complained that she couldn't walk in the high heels, so that was it!"

On our way back to the car, Douglas asked, "What are you doing tomorrow?"

"Do you want to do something together?"

"Yes, what do you want to do?"

"If you ask me," I said, "then I have a thousand ideas of what to do. We could go to Maastricht, to see the winter lights, or to Bernkastel-Kues, or go running, or go biking, or go shopping in Luxembourg, or ..."

"Maastricht would be perfect!"

"So let's go to Maastricht! I love the Netherlands!"

"And thanks for buying me this gingerbread heart. I'll only look at what's written on it when I'm back home."

I said with a smile, "Yes, please, you do that."

Later, Douglas wrote: "Ich liebe dich auch."

The heart had read: "Ich liebe dich."

Saturday, 5 December 2020 – Maastricht

Douglas: "Good morning, dear Julia."

"Good morning dear Douglas :)   meet at 2 pm at the Decathlon car park ok? :)"

Douglas: "Sure."

"Am happy."

Douglas: "Me too. I'm happy with you."

Douglas and I went to Maastricht, a two-hour drive through the Belgium Ardennes. The highway is mainly straight and the border to the Netherlands opens up to more flat countryside with fruit and vegetable farms, which is typical for the Netherlands.

As expected, the Christmas market in Maastricht was cancelled because of the coronavirus but they had put the Christmas lights all over town. Shops were open, as well as the usual antiques market and the fish stands, where we ate a fish dish. The only thing was that we had to eat it standing up at special socially-distanced coronavirus tables and we also made sure we were under cover. This was to protect the fish from the seagulls, who are well-known fish thieves in the city.

Douglas and I went through Maastricht city centre, over the bridge to the other side, with lovely views of the sunset over the Maas river There was the red star lit up on the other side of the river. We continued over the next bridge, a pedestrian and bike bridge over the Maas, back to the Groote Markt, passing by the Basilica of Saint Servatius and the Dominican church, which had been converted into a bookstore. The Groote Markt usually hosts the Christmas market but was now empty.

"So," asked Douglas, "what are you doing tomorrow?"

"Do you want to do something together?"

"Yes, I really enjoy being with you. It's such a pleasure. Yes, how about in the afternoon? Do you want to go biking, or hiking, or whatever would make you happy?"

"It's Christmas time and we still can go biking later once Christmas is over, why don't we go to Bernkastel-Kues to see what they are offering there to replace their Christmas market?"

"Yes, with pleasure. I'll look it up on the internet."

"Oh, yes, I'm so happy that the two of us have met thanks to the coronavirus. Without it we would never have met. There is some good in this crisis."

"Indeed, me too, I'm so happy that we met. I like spending time with you so much, it is a real pleasure."

Saint Nicholas Day – 6 December 2020 – Bernkastel-Kues

It was 'Nikolaus-Tag' – Saint Nicholas Day. Louis taught his fitness class on Facebook and over eighty people attended. This was a good way to start the day.

Douglas came to pick me up to go to Bernkastel-Kues. Although the Christmas market had indeed been cancelled, there were still some stands, down on the main riverfront road, separated to allow social distancing. We had 'Flammkuchen' and some alcohol-free Glühwein. In the town centre they had put up stands purely as decoration, with nobody and nothing inside them. Buildings were lit with lights that changed from red to purple, orange and green, and spelling out festive messages. Otherwise, all other traditions were cancelled, such as the customary torchlight swim, the Saint Nicholas parade, the singing, and the distribution of chocolate – all cancelled. We talked with some locals who said that this Christmas was an economic disaster, with measures not justifying the outcome.

We went all the way up to the castle for its stunning views. We took pictures and had pictures taken of us and a man who was taking pictures said 'with a kiss.' So we kissed there with the magnificent view for the first time. It was a 'kiss at the castle'.

On our way back to the car, we held hands and talked.

"I am so happy being with you," Douglas said, "I think about you all the time. We make a nice couple. What are you doing tomorrow? Are you very busy?"

"Yes, I am always very busy, but we have our Distance Fitness at my place in the evening. If you want to join us you are very welcome."

"I'll be there!"

Monday, 7 December 2020

"This coronavirus pandemic will not be the last one," Jordan was telling me, "We'll live through more of these viruses, I heard scientists say, with an economic collapse predicted in twenty years or so from now. All the different viruses will kill about two-thirds of the current population and one of the countries where to survive best is... ? Guess which one?"

"Well, I really don't know. You tell me!" I said.

"Canada!"

"Why?"

"Because Canada is one of the biggest countries on earth, has a relatively small population and has some of the largest water resources."

Distance Fitness is unstoppable

Before the Distance Fitness class I told everyone, "Yesterday was Saint Nicholas day, so today I brought you all a Nicholas chocolate. And also, may I present Douglas? He is attending Distance Fitness for the first time today."

The music began and we started the routine but not without much conversation.

Peter: "Let's check if our shoelaces are well done up."

Jordan: "I have a joke for later!"

Peter: "Everybody smile!"

Jasmine: "Julia, I brought you a 'Boxemännchen'. Hope it tastes good."

Peter: "Do we do the left leg first, am I doing it right?"

Douglas: "Ah, all this movement, I am not good at it. Which leg first?"

Jasmine: "Don't worry, just try to follow."

Jordan: "What did you say, I cannot hear you!"

Claire: "We're enjoying ourselves, all you need to know!"

Peter: "Let's take some pictures of us all!"

Douglas: "I also have a joke or two!"

Jordan: "Good, let's hear it!"

And so the evening went on, we exercised in the cold and the dark and with some really good music, kept talking while we were doing it and, most of all, enjoyed ourselves.

From that day on, Douglas and I were inseparable.

In the week of 7 December 2020, Great Britain started vaccinations against the coronavirus.
In the week of 14 December 2020, the USA started vaccinations.
In Europe, new lockdowns and curfews were declared.
Germany decided to close all shops on 11 December.
France had a curfew from eight p.m. starting from 15 December.
The Netherlands decided to introduce a lockdown on 15 December, shutting down all shops and museums for one month, meaning over Christmas and New Year.
Italy, on 18 December, decided on a stricter lockdown over Christmas.
Belgium required a valid – meaning not older than 48 hours – negative coronavirus test for all non-residents entering the country.
India started vaccinating the entire population on 18 December 2020.

Christmas and beyond

Christmas was almost upon us. This was a different Christmas than all other Christmases before. Douglas and I enjoyed Distance Fitness with Jordan, Jasmine, Peter and Carmen, in the dark and in the rain. We ate Christmas cake after class in the rain. The only topics of conversation seemed to be the pandemic and what we were doing for Christmas. Douglas, because he lived in France, had to leave early to be back home before curfew. As he was leaving, he would open his car window and call out, "See you tomorrow, I love you!"

A new coronavirus variant was discovered in the UK and in South Africa, resulting in a complete lockdown of London, the UK and South Africa. All flights from there were cancelled. The Netherlands was the first to stop all flights from London.

---

24 and 25 December 2020

For Christmas Eve, Patricia, Douglas and I went to church. This year, the service was held outside in the cold and with social distancing. However, the priest, and the congregation celebrated Christmas in a festive way.

On Christmas Day, the three of us, after a festive lunch, went Nordic Walking together in the forest.

During the walk Douglas said, "Climate change makes me afraid much more than the coronavirus. I am not afraid of coronavirus. But fifteen degrees at Christmas is not normal. The ice in the Antarctic is melting. Huge mountains of ice are melting and nobody is doing anything. Soon, the Netherlands will be inundated. Key West, the Maldives and many other places will all disappear into the sea."

I added to his thought, "Deforestation in the Amazon region has never been as intense as this year. Nobody is doing much against it, it's all about coronavirus. If they invested as much money into environmental protection as they do into coronavirus measures, things would be much better. But no, they don't care. Nobody talks about Greta Thundberg or 'Fridays for future' anymore! Where are they? Why does nobody do anything about protection of the natural world?

"Look at the low level of the water in the lake we just passed," Patricia said, "Normally it's filled up but now it is at least two 2 metres lower, maybe even more. With deforestation in the Amazon progressing, the rain will completely stop here. This is the real tragedy, not the coronavirus. I refuse to wear my mask at home with you. Nobody has anything and I am not afraid of the virus."

I said, "Probably disinfecting your hands all the time and living in a sterile world will kill us, because our immune system will be so weak that we will die from the smallest virus or dirt. All of this is complete nonsense."

"There are a few books you might like to read with criticism of this and the nonsense of the system. What do you think the world will be like after this pandemic?" Douglas asked.

I continued, "This is a complete reset. The future of education is online. The speed of the development of online education has increased dramatically. Instead of taking years, as some people said it would, it took one day. The future is online. Everything will be online. Young people, and not just young people, are online with friends worldwide. They don't travel in planes, they don't go to hotels, they don't meet in person in boring meetings. They organise Zoom meetings, and there is no travel, no plane or train to take, no hotel, no lunch, no dinner, nothing, just a one-hour hour online Zoom meeting. This is the new reality. Nobody will want to go back to the world of business trips, or holiday trips, like there were before March last year. This is a complete reset. The world will be different."

"Those who are flexible enough to adapt will survive," Douglas said, "This is another revolution. It is a crisis like the 1928 economic crisis, but today the stock market is computerised and many trades are carried out by algorithms. Do you think, people will travel again to see the pyramids in Egypt or the Taj Mahal in India? Probably they will just visit them online on their screens, comfortably seated in their living rooms. On the other hand, this is also a big challenge for many couples if they live in a small apartment, with kids, and have to combine working at home with home schooling, all from the small apartment, with a noisy street outside. The importance of what we do and how we live in the home is growing."

"Nothing will be the same," I agreed, "This is a complete reset. Those who are flexible will succeed, those who stick to their former habits will fail."

"Luckily we always have been flexible in our family," Patricia said, "It is about 'Individualism' and about 'Uncertainty Avoidance', this is where your studies around Geert Hofstede and his cultural dimension come to the fore. The discussion goes on, and they remain as current as ever."

There was another lockdown in Luxembourg. This one shut down all non-food shops, starting 26 December, with the curfew starting at nine at night instead of eleven. In France and Italy the curfew started at eight, but in Italy there was a complete lockdown over Christmas and all non-essential movement out of the house was forbidden.

Christmas message from Douglas

"My darling, I love you so much, I think about you all the time! Merry Christmas to you! My Christmas present is you! We will spend so many wonderful moments together, we are so lucky that we met. I love you! It is wonderful to be so much in love! It's been a long time since I have been so much in love. I love you!"

Vaccinations had already started in the USA and the UK but in Europe they only started on Sunday 27 December. This was a concerted action and Luxembourg started on 28 December. Most countries would start seriously vaccinating in the beginning of January 2021.

---

28 December 2020 to 3 January 2021 – Amsterdam

On Tuesday, 28 December, Douglas and I went to Amsterdam, for a three-day bike tour. We decided to extend it to take in New Year's day and the weekend. We spent New Year's eve in Amsterdam, enjoying the warm sunny days and eating the Kibbeling at the beach. We visited North Holland by bike: from Amsterdam to Haarlem, Bloemendal, Zandvort, Noordwjik, Katwjik, and also to Bergen, Bergen-aan-Zee, Callantsog. On New Year's Day, we went to Texel, taking the ferry boat from Den Helder, eating Haring in the rain, drinking hot chocolate at a take-away and chatting with other cyclists.

This is where Douglas said, "Next time we'll come to Texel, we'll do the skydive you did last summer. I want to jump it together with you, from 13,000 feet. Seeing the earth from there in free fall must be most impressive."

"For now, we will go swimming in the North Sea," I replied, "This is the New Year tradition here."

"Okay," said Douglas. And off we went for a dip in the cold waters of the North Sea, a short dip indeed and very refreshing. Some young Dutch people lent us their towels after the swim. Later in the evening, just as the sun was setting, we had vegetable soup with bread and hot chocolate at a beach take-away stand.

"This is the best hot chocolate ever," exclaimed Douglas, "Well, the one on Texel was also excellent, but here at the beach with the sunset, unforgettable! I love you, I love you so much, you are adorable, you are my darling!"

Despite the pandemic and its threats to health, social life, job security and the world in general, the New Year started with cycling, love and tenderness.

January 2021

Since the day we had first met, Douglas and I were inseparable. Every day, we met and went jogging or walking and talked about many things but especially about the future.

"There are so many topics to discuss," suggested Douglas, "The size of the economic impact of this pandemic cannot be foreseen. I wonder about the banks with all the unpaid loans coming up. So many people are unable to pay their debts. Look at all these shops closed, all the restaurants are closed. How will they survive? Are governments worldwide supposed to pay for all this? And then there's climate change! Online living, online working, online finance, online everything, the future is digitalisation."

"Another topic," I added, "is why don't they vaccinate people? They have the vaccine ready and don't vaccinate us. I cannot believe how much time they are taking. It's terrible!"

Joe Biden was sworn in as 46th President of the United States of America, together with Kamala Harris as Vice-President.
The Netherlands introduced a curfew from nine in the evening to half past four in the morning. This measure led to demonstrations and violence.
French leaders were contemplating the reintroduction of a complete lockdown, just like in March 2020. In the end, they decided against such a move. However, France is running very much behind its vaccination schedule.
Across Europe, vaccinations had not been delivered as they had been promised.
More infectious and more dangerous new variants of the coronavirus were cropping up all over the world.

During a Distance Fitness class, Jasmine, Jordan, Peter, Tony, Douglas, Claire and I decided to go and see a movie entitled 'Summerland', just like my name. In the film, Summerland is a heavenly place with castles in the sky and happiness, love and childhood dreams.

After we had seen it and were leaving the cinema, I turned to everyone and said, "Let's make a movie out of our book! We will all play our own roles!"

"We are ready!" my friends exclaimed.

Douglas added, "We'll all go together to Texel for the skydive for the movie, yes!"

February 2021

Nordic Walking

Since November, we had been Nordic Walking nearly every day with Melissa, one of my friends. We had done over 520 kilometres by the end of February 2021. We went walking in all weather, including in the snow and the rain. Whatever the weather, warm, cold or wet, the three of us went uphill and downhill, mainly in Luxembourg city, through some of the capital's prettiest spots.

Valentine's Day

Compared to the previous year, when I had been all alone, a very different Valentine's Day awaited me this year. This year, Douglas arrived with a bouquet of red roses and took me hiking along the famous Saarschleife trail in Germany. Once we had completed the difficult uphill walk, we were rewarded with stunning views.

In February, with the days getting longer, warmer and sunnier, on other occasions, Douglas and I went to many different places. We got around mainly on our racing bikes but also made good use of our Nordic Walking poles, going to Remich for the bike path along the Moselle river, or to Saarbrücken along the Saar river, to Saarburg as well as to Mersch, Mamer, Clémency, Garnich, Hespérange, and many other places.

"Your birthday will be soon, what do you wish for your birthday?" I asked Douglas, who replied without hesitation, "The Netherlands, Amsterdam, biking with you! And on my birthday, we will go for a swim in the North Sea!"

"Oh, yes, that's fabulous, we will book the hotel and go biking in North Holland, perfect!"

Oliver – what a surprise

While jogging with Douglas in March I received a text message that read "Hi Julia!"

I said to Douglas, "Look here, you remember Oliver, from my book? I met him one year ago, here he is back, what a surprise. We met on Meetyourlove long before you."

"What does he want?" Douglas asked.

"I don't know, let's see what he has to say."

I wrote back to Oliver: "How are you, Oliver?"

Oliver replied: "Am fine, just working from home like everybody else. And you?"

While jogging with Douglas, I decided to wait before writing a reply.

Three days after this exchange, I received a message from Oliver asking, "Do you want to go biking today?"

I decided to call him. "Hi Oliver. How are you?" I asked, "After such a long time, it's been one year that we last spoke. You want to go biking with me today? If you are open minded, we can go together for a bike ride, because I have met somebody on Meetyourlove, and you? Did you find a woman?"

"I had some serious health issues, no coronavirus, but heart surgery, serious heart surgery last year, and no, I didn't meet anybody. Well, okay, I did meet a woman and we spent two months together, but she left me because she had a big choice in men. I am open minded, so, yes, we could go meet in Remich and cycle together, the three of us. We could then come to my place and eat Flammkuchen, what do you think?"

"I'll ask Douglas and see what he says and let you know."

I called Douglas and asked him, "How open minded are you? Would you accept going cycling and having Flammkuchen with a man I met before you on Meetyourlove?"

"Yes, why not? Let's do it!"

This is how the three of us met on a Sunday on the bike path in Remich, for biking and later Flammkuchen at Oliver's place.

I gave Oliver a copy of my first book and told him that he would be part of the second one too, and also in the movie. We planned to meet again for pizza next time and a bike ride to Trier together.

Gérard

"We could go to the Müllerthal! Please, let's go all together. Please, it would be my pleasure if we could go together with your new boyfriend. I am open minded. Let's go there, I love the Müllerthal. For my rehabilitation, this is the best therapy."

Raphaël

"My beautiful Julia, he is a lucky man, your Douglas. I would have liked to have a girlfriend like you, but I live too far away from you, so he is very lucky. However, if one day you come to my region, or I come to Luxembourg, it would be my pleasure if we could go cycling together, the three of us, if this is okay. Yesterday, I had especially good legs, pulling the entire group behind me against the wind. I like it when it's difficult and my legs burn from the effort. Hope to see you and your new, lucky man one day in person. Keep safe, stay healthy, am going to work now, while you sleep. This is no life, to work at nights, but it's the only solution for me to go cycling during the day, while working at nights. Your Raphaël."

Mid-March 2021 Biking - The Netherlands

Douglas and I went biking in the Netherlands... to celebrate his birthday...

Mid-End March 2021

... and Patricia's birthday...

... and one year of Distance Fitness.

While vaccination procedures and closure policies continued to be chaotic – with Germany announcing another severe lockdown over the Easter festivities, only to revoke them the day after – this book comes slowly but surely to an end. I would now like to invite all readers to read "Douglas's story" on the following pages, right after this chapter, as well as two short afterwords, one by Bernard and the other by Jordan.

Douglas's story

An Italian summer

By Douglas B.

Last summer was marked by disappointment in love and I decided to overcome it. It was the end of a beautiful love story that had started really well.

Love stories usually end badly. My beautiful brunette had decided to return to her previous lover. At the same time, I was lucky enough to be invited to a friend's house in Italy, so I had a pretty nice summer.

I love the atmosphere of these little Italian villages. In the evenings in the sensual heat of summer, we rebuilt the world around a good glass of wine and some dishes of pasta or fritto misto.

When I returned back home, I made the decision to register on the MeetyourLove dating site. I had the opportunity to chat online with different women and then I had some unlikely encounters.

Elisabeth

The first, Elisabeth, whom I met in the Moselle department in France, was a charming person: pretty, tall and blonde who did the same job as me. She was smiling and relaxed, but I had a little trouble understanding her real intentions.

I saw her a second time when we had lunch in Belgium on a terrace in the sun. We walked next to a lake and planned to meet again a third time.

I never saw her again because she suddenly stopped exchanging messages.

I presumed that she had surely met someone more beautiful, richer, younger and smarter.

Marie

The second encounter was strange.

Her name was Marie and she insisted on meeting me. She was nervous and a little lost in her thoughts. She confessed that she was extremely traumatized by the atmosphere and constraints around the pandemic.

Indeed, she was afraid of losing her job, her mother was sick and her social relations were at a standstill. She had completely isolated herself for fear of the virus. Our conversations were not too positive I did not want to see her again, even if she was rather pretty.

I wished for her to meet someone more beautiful, richer, younger and smarter.

Estelle

Estelle was a beautiful brunette who had an important job in a pharmaceutical lab. She was working remotely during the confinement. She had free time and she invited me to have a coffee at her house.

I realized that this person had family problems, especially with her children, and that she was having a bad time with her recent divorce. I also realized that she wanted to take action quickly from a sexual point of view, you know what I mean.

I decided to go home.

I wished for her to meet someone more beautiful, richer, younger and smarter.

Julia

I met Julia in October on the website. I was seduced at first by her broad, confident smile and later by her strange and indefinable accent.

We exchanged messages to get to know each other. We discussed the usual things: professional situation, family situation and relationship status. I immediately felt like I was dealing with someone open minded, clever and very dynamic.

She was also very curious and a little suspicious. She wanted to know my last name to google me and check my age and my career path on the web. So she found out my real age since I hadn't told the truth about it.

She told me that she was looking for someone younger. I could easily understand it.

Our exchanges therefore stopped.

Of course, I wished for her to meet someone more beautiful, richer, younger and smarter.

A surprise and a happy end

At the end of November, I received an unexpected phone call from Julia who wanted to get back in touch with me. I immediately thought that her encounters on the site had not been satisfactory or she had been left by a potential lover.

She had still not met someone more beautiful, richer, younger and smarter.

Why was she still interested in me?

Two days later we met in person in Luxembourg city for a walk and since then we haven't left each other. I didn't think I could fall in love with a woman who rarely goes to the hairdresser, goes to church and mends her own socks.

And since then I love that little Luxembourg stream... the Pétrusse.

In addition to the Distance Fitness, bicycling and ice skating – she is my idol – we decided to get high together ...I don't mean sexually or with drugs. I mean we plan to go skydiving in the Netherlands on the island of Texel.

Douglas B.

Afterword by Bernard

Now I know why they call it the 'Grand'-Duchy of Luxembourg

6,500 kilometres. Yes, Julia and Carl cycled 6,500 kilometres in Luxembourg in 2020, the year of the coronavirus pandemic. I didn't know that the place was that big, nor that one could bike so many kilometres without exiting the country. Now I understand why they call it the 'Grand'-Duchy of Luxembourg.

Despite this painful period of time, with all its closures and prohibitions, she has managed to meet many men, most of whom were not 'officially' available, men who wanted to 'play.' It took her much time and energy to sift through extremely ambitious men till she hit the lottery and met with a man who was honest.... except for lying about his age.

Despite her looking for a younger man, Julia ended up with Douglas because all other 'candidates' lied about almost everything, from their marital status ("I am in the process of getting a divorce"), to age, income, organizational position, and even posting 'wish to look like' photos on their dating webpage. It is unbelievable how far men are willing to go to 'catch their fish' – one had posted an old picture of Brad Pitt with the hope he wouldn't be caught out.

While others were playing games, Julia did not lose her focus and managed to publish her first book "Love in Times of Coronavirus", in paper, in e-book and in audiobook forms. Wait, there is more to come. After this second book

Julia is planning to take her story to Hollywood and to make a movie with the temporary name "Alter! Nein, wirklich, wie alt bist du?" I am sure that when I watch this movie I would not only be able to learn more about the 'Grand'-Duchy of Luxembourg, with its famous Pétrusse valley Douglas is talking about, but also about dating and lying in days of Corona and beyond.

Hope you enjoyed your reading.

Bernard M.

Afterword by Jordan

The Host

While attending Julia's webinars for her university, eagerly taking pictures and videos, at first I noticed her only incidentally: the host. Initially, my eyes were on the webinar presenter. However, when reviewing my pictures and videos, there she was again: the host. The more I looked at her pictures, the more she came to my mind. She was always there with a professional smile. Her eyes perfectly lined in black, her lips coloured in a red, so red it struck me, her hair combed back.

From that moment on, every time I attended Julia's webinars, online for coronavirus reasons, my concentration was more on the host than on the presenter. With some ruse I even succeeded in getting the host's phone number, a happy day for me and I started writing her messages.

The host always speaks in a friendly professional way, introducing the presenter and the organizers, unmuting participants with a friendly but decisive manner, asking participants to speak, then to speak up, or to write their questions in the Q&A sections, reading out loud their contributions. The host became for me reason for participating in each and every webinar, taking pictures and videos and making her happy by sending them to her.

This was one of my contributions to happiness in coronavirus times: making the host happy.

Jordan

THE END